The Parting Glass

Anthony J. Bulnes

The Parting Glass

Olympia Publishers
London

www.olympiapublishers.com
OLYMPIA PAPERBACK EDITION

Copyright © Anthony J. Bulnes 2022

The right of Anthony J. Bulnes to be identified as author of
this work has been asserted in accordance with sections 77 and 78 of
the Copyright, Designs and Patents Act 1988.

All Rights Reserved

No reproduction, copy or transmission of this publication
may be made without written permission.
No paragraph of this publication may be reproduced,
copied or transmitted save with the written permission of the publisher,
or in accordance with the provisions
of the Copyright Act 1956 (as amended).

Any person who commits any unauthorised act in relation to
this publication may be liable to criminal
prosecution and civil claims for damage.

A CIP catalogue record for this title is
available from the British Library.

ISBN: 978-1-80074-551-3

This is a work of fiction.
Names, characters, places and incidents originate from the writer's
imagination. Any resemblance to actual persons, living or dead, is
purely coincidental.

First Published in 2022

Olympia Publishers
Tallis House
2 Tallis Street
London
EC4Y 0AB

Printed in Great Britain

Dedication

I dedicate this book to my mother, Carol. Without you, I would never have had a chance to tell my stories.

Acknowledgements

Thank you to my girlfriend, Tichynna, for encouraging me to tell my story and serving as my backbone throughout this whole process.

Act I
Chapter 1
What Kind of Heart Doesn't Look Back?

The night is calm. A cool, slow breeze brushes up against the windows, creating a blissful whistle in the somber sky. The stars give off a brilliant glow that lights up even the most illuminated city. The nightlife never seemed so peaceful, so perfect.

For one couple, it is a horrid nightmare. As the rest of the world sleeps during the beautiful twilight, Aiden and his fiancée, Skylar, are in a shouting match that puts the heaviest weight boxing title fights to shame. Though the darkness outside is nothing but harmonious, the fluorescent inside is anything but. The two go back and forth not caring who can hear them or if they hurt each other's feelings.

Their daughter, Marie, is down the hall pretending to sleep. She is a wonderful toddler with luscious, long brunette curls. Her skin is pasty white just like her parents, and her smile is as bright as the sun itself. She's usually all smiles, but not tonight. As tears run down her beautiful face, Marie knows she has been displeased for a long time. She has to hear her parents try to outdo each other with insults and hurtful slurs. There hasn't been a quiet night in their home for as long as she can remember. At only four years old, Marie has come to understand that her parents are nothing more than distasteful human beings with no regard for those who love them. While they fight, she places her favorite stuffed dog to her ear to block out the ugly yells. To no avail; she brings her puppy down to eye level.

"Do you think they will ever stop, Everest?" she asks her toy Dalmatian.

Sadly, Marie receives no response. In her mind, if she closes her eyes tight enough, she will be able to go back to sleep and when she wakes up, the nightmare will be just that. As each second passes, Marie grips onto Everest tighter and tighter while she shuts her eyes harder and harder.

"Promise me, Everest. Promise me we will never be like Mommy and Daddy."

The sudden sound of shattering glass echoes throughout Marie's room, confusing her. It is something she has never heard before. She is used to the curses and high-pitched shrieks, but not this. Tonight is something completely new, and completely terrifying. Now, with her eyes wide open and her brain more awake than it should be at this ungodly hour, Marie tosses aside her furry pink blanket, quickly scurries out of bed and hops into her slippers. Just as she is about to walk away from her bed, she reaches over to snatch Everest and places him under her gently trembling arm. Petrified of what else she might hear, Marie slowly drags her feet against her floor in her shadowy room. She heads toward the small glimmer of light coming from outside her bedroom door, which she left slightly ajar.

With Everest in one hand, Marie reaches out and slowly opens her bedroom door with the other. Usually, her door lets out a clear and distinct squeal, but tonight it seems as though this door knows it must remain as mute as her stuffed pup. Yet with the way Aiden and Skylar are at each other's throats, a squeaky door probably wouldn't matter. Slowly down the hall, the young girl tiptoes her way towards her screaming parents. Just before reaching their bedroom door, Marie easily slides up against the wall just before the doorway frame. She softly brushes her face along the side of the arch and faintly pushes her face forward, just enough that she is able to peek through without anyone detecting her presence.

There, Marie sees her mother down on her knees while clutching her stomach. She's almost a spitting image of her daughter, except her lips are just a bit fuller and her hair is a glorious shade of dirty blonde. Usually full of love and hope, she notices her mother's face is crimson red and her eyes, usually a perfect dough brown, are bloodshot and full of despair. A woman whom she views to be so strong and so beautiful is now a broken mess. She sees her mother pound the wooden floor with both fists while she looks up and shouts, "So, who is she, Aiden?"

Marie then slightly turns her head and notices her father, with a look of complete disbelief, standing over her mother with his arms crossed. She watches him standing in his typical tank top and sweatpants. He's not a fairly tall man but his muscles make him well proportioned. He also has the most gentle, hazel eyes with hair similar to his daughter's. Only his hair isn't in long locks but in a short fade.

Aiden places one hand over his rugged beard and caresses it rather roughly before responding.

"We've been over this, Skylar. I'm not going to repeat myself over and over again to you."

"I don't understand."

"What don't you understand? Tell me."

"I don't understand how you can do this to me, to our family."

"What family, Sky? Me and you playing house, pretending we're something we're not? Something we will never be? We haven't truly been together for a long time."

"How can you say this to me? Has everything been a lie?"

Skylar asks, releasing a horrific sob.

Before answering, Aiden pauses and looks down at Skylar. For a brief second, he begins to feel guilty. Anyone that knows Aiden knows guilt is not his commonly visited sentiment. He quickly shakes it out and responds, "No, not everything has been a lie. You wouldn't understand."

"What's to understand, Aiden? The way I see it, it's black and white. Be a man for once and tell me everything you have to say, dammit."

"I have nothing left to say to you at this point."

Skylar begins to catch her breath. Her sobs transform into heavy puffs of anger. She looks up at Aiden's breathtaking hazel eyes. Eyes that once made her melt into a river of love now make her want to rip every brunette-colored hair by the follicles off his scalp.

"Just tell me this: did you sleep with her?" Skylar demands.

Stunned by her question, Aiden looks down, hopeless and guilt-ridden. He shakes his head while his body begins to quiver in fear. He knows she already knows the answer, but for some reason he just can't bring himself to say it.

"AIDEN!" she shouts, redirecting his attention to her. "Did you sleep with her? It's a simple question. Yes, or no?"

"I'm not answering that," he says.

"Why not? Because you did, didn't you?"

"I'm not saying that."

"Then tell me what you are saying, because from my point of view, you're too chicken shit to admit anything to my face."

Aiden just stands there. He refuses to answer. Not because he wants to continue lying, but because he feels that avoiding the question could make the night end faster.

"AIDEN!" Skylar shouts even louder.

Aiden looks at Skylar, confused. He cannot understand why she continues to nag.

"SPEAK!"

"YES! Okay! Yes. I did it," he reluctantly answers. "I slept with her."

No sooner are the words out of Aiden's mouth, the love that was left in Skylar's heart tears to shreds. Her entire world crashes. Her stomach instantly drops to the floor. While her lungs try to grasp for air, her brain attempts to comprehend Aiden's betrayal. Even though she already knew the truth, actually hearing him say it terrifies her. It is a dagger to the heart. After what seems like a lifetime, Skylar begins to collect her thoughts and her words. She has come up with one thousand responses, but only one seems right.

"I need you to get out of my house. Collect your things, Aiden, and get out."

"Your house? When did this become your house?" Aiden questions.

Without thinking twice, Skylar rises intimidatingly from her knees and stomps her way to Aiden, placing her nose a centimeter away from his.

"The day you stuck that thing," she points to Aiden's waist, "in another woman."

"I have every right to be here, just like you."

"No. No, you don't. Not any more."

"Sky—"

"Don't. Don't 'Sky' me. You make me sick."

Aiden extends his arm out to console her, but she swiftly pushes him aside.

"And do NOT dare to touch me."

Aiden takes a small step backwards, placing his hands in the air and surrendering.

"Now pack your stuff and go."

Unable to understand what's happening in front of her eyes, Marie finally steps forward from out of the hallway shadows and into her parents' room.

"Mommy?" she asks.

Startled and confused, Skylar rapidly swings her head in her daughter's direction.

"Marie, baby, what are you doing out of bed?" Skylar asks while brushing the tears running down her rose-colored cheeks away from her face.

"I couldn't sleep any more. What's going on? Is Daddy leaving?"

"Oh baby, come here," Skylar says. She opens her arms instructing Marie to come fill the emptiness. Without hesitation, Marie scurries over, and her mother picks her up. Now eye-to-eye with her mother, she takes her gentle hand and swipes her mother's left-over tears.

"Why are you crying, Mommy? Is it because of something Daddy did?"

Amazed at how much her daughter can understand, she decides to be honest.

"Don't tell her that. You're going to put thoughts in her head," Aiden exclaims.

"Well, maybe you should have thought about that before you did what you did," Skylar replies sarcastically.

"What did you do, Daddy?"

"Nothing, baby. This is grown-up time. Let's get you back to bed, okay?"

"Daddy decided he doesn't want to be with Mommy any more. Daddy has decided he wants to be with another woman,"

Skylar says full of disdain and hurt.

"What the hell is wrong with you? She's four. You can't tell her things like that!"

"Like I said, you should've thought about that before." Skylar pauses before turning towards Marie and looking into her worried eyes. "I'm her mother. I'll never lie to her. I wouldn't expect you to understand. You have never had a mother."

Aiden's expression changes dramatically. The tension in the room grows ten times over. He can feel his face and ears getting hot. His blood starts to boil. His teeth squeeze so hard together that someone a mile away could see their definition. His right hand, balls into a tight fist, causing his veins to bulge. He feels his face blazing. His left hand hastily grabs his clenched fist and clasps it down in hopes that it will stop him from making a stupid decision.

"What did you just say to me?" Aiden asks, grinding his teeth.

"You heard me. You can't understand a child's feelings for their mother because you never had one!" Skylar replies with horrid satisfaction.

Aiden uses all his willpower to not leap at Skylar and wipe the sadistic grin off her face.

"You are lucky that you're not a man!" Aiden says.

"Why? Are you gonna hit me, Aiden? Come on then, big man. Hit me. Show us the man you truly are," she replies, tempting him.

"You're not worth my time, Sky. You're just upset that I don't want you any more. Get over yourself."

"Is that what your mother said right before—"

Aiden jolts toward Skylar, grabbing her wrist tightly. She notices his red pupils dying to spill out. It takes everything in him and more to hold back a mighty blow to the side of her face.

"Mention her one more time and I promise you that Marie isn't the only one I'm putting back to sleep."

Skylar smiles, knowing she struck his final nerve. She has him right where she wants him. Instead of replying or giving in to his request, she simply tugs her arm from his grip and places Marie down.

"Do it then. Hit me," Skylar dares Aiden.

For half a second, Aiden considers it. He knows it'll make him feel good for the moment, but it will be a short-lived happiness. But that's not who he is. It's not what he does. He just thinks to himself, what kind of man could strike a female in front of his child? He turns towards Marie, releasing Skylar from his grip. Several inches away, his daughter stands, shaking. Her face is as pale as the winter snow and her eyes fill with more water than any ocean.

"Marie," he calls out, reaching for her.

"Don't you dare touch her!" Skylar shouts, shoving Aiden away.

Assuredly, Aiden's reflexes kick in and in less than a second, he finds himself shoving back with tremendous force. Feeling the impact of the thrust, Skylar stumbles back, knocking Marie down to the ground. Marie's body hits the floor with a loud thud. Her high-pitched scream triggers Aiden to dive by her side.

"Marie!" Aiden shouts.

Unable to move as fast as he did, Skylar follows.

"Oh my God, my baby!" Skylar says worriedly.

Skylar clutches onto Marie and shoves Aiden to the side.

"Get the hell away from us!" she stresses while crying alongside her daughter. "This is all your fault. Everything is your fault!"

"I didn't mean—" Aiden begins to say before he is interrupted.

"GET OUT!"

"I have to see if she's all right."

"NOW!"

Unsure of what to say or what to do, Aiden complies. He rises to his feet in disgust. He can't help but feel self-disapproval after everything that has happened. Shaking his head, he takes one last look around his pumpkin-painted room. He glimpses over the pictures hanging on the walls and embraces that this is it. He realizes he must let go of his memories, from his favorite television to the fan on the ceiling. He knows this isn't his home and it quite possibly never was. Aiden walks over to his jacket and snatches it off his computer chair with soreness. He looks down at his daughter and her mother in sorrow.

"For what it's worth, I truly am sorry." Aiden pauses. "I'm sorry, baby," he apologizes to his daughter.

"We don't care, Aiden. Just leave already."

"Okay... I'll go."

Aiden slowly vanishes into the darkness. He takes one last look at his broken family and shares a final tear with them. The sound of the door slamming shut echoes throughout their well-furnished home, but it is at that moment that it never felt emptier.

Act I
Chapter 2
Make the World Brand New

Six months later, Aiden finds himself fiercely attached to his best friend, Kenneth. Day in and day out he has been trying to help Aiden get over his sorrows, but tonight is a little more special. Kenneth finally gets Aiden out of his apartment and into a finely tailored grey suit with an effortlessly pressed black buttoned-down shirt. They go out and end up at one of the city's most extravagant bars.

Both men, dressed exceptionally well, sit side by side at the bar, which is a beautifully carved golden-brown marble. The background is dimly lit in a perfect combination of orange and blue. The tables are flawlessly put together with royal chairs and tablecloths to match, topped with a candle for elegance.

Aiden, with a beer in hand, takes a quick glimpse towards the back of the room before nudging his friend and saying, "So, what do I owe the pleasure of you bringing me to a place like this?"

Kenneth, who's been Aiden's best friend since high school, is a short and cuddly gentleman with a beard that is three times as scruffy compared to Aiden's, who looks like he just started puberty with the peach fuzz growing out of his chin and cheeks. Kenneth is best described as a living teddy bear, not only in color and fluffiness, but because he is one of the most soft and warming souls that anyone could ever meet.

"Owe me? You don't owe me a thing. I thought it was about

time we got you out of those nasty sweats and into something that better suits you, so to speak," Kenneth replies.

"It's been to my knowledge that you would like to get me out of anything," Aiden says with a wink and smile.

"That's... not wrong." Kenneth and Aiden chuckle.

"In all seriousness though, I figured you needed a few drinks and a real night out," Kenneth adds.

"Sounds like you're just trying to get me into bed, Kenneth Sanchez."

"Hey... whatever happens, happens." Both men laugh.

Aiden, once again, takes a look in the same direction as earlier. Kenneth quickly realizes what is grabbing his friend's attention. He turns to Aiden and asks, "How's about you stop looking, actually go over there and talk to the girl?"

"What girl?" Aiden asks, still staring.

"The one you're giving stalker eyes to, dummy."

"I am not giving stalker eyes," he says, finally looking away.

"Could have fooled me," Kenneth spits out, taking a sip of his cocktail.

Unsure of what to do, Aiden slightly angles his head towards the back of the room and shakes it while gesturing for another beer. He knows that six months has been long enough. Then again, maybe he might be going too fast. His facial expressions easily give off that he is currently battling in his own mind.

"Dude... you're thinking way too loud. What is it?" Kenneth asks.

"It's nothing," Aiden responds now looking at his friend.

"We haven't lied to one another since the tenth grade. Let's not start tonight, Aiden."

"It's just that... don't you think it may be too soon to be talking to other girls?"

"Too soon? Okay, who are you and what have you done with my heterosexual best friend that secretly wants me?"

"Ha ha, very funny." Aiden takes another gulp of beer. "I'm serious though."

"Dude, you're going over there to talk to the girl, not to sleep with her. Come on."

"I guess you're right."

"Of course I'm right. Now get that fine ass up and march on over there, unless of course you are indeed into me."

"You're never going to give up, are you?" Aiden laughs.

"Nope... never."

Aiden confidently stands up from his stool, takes one last drink of his liquid courage and begins to make his way over to the woman he cannot seem to take his eyes off. There, sitting in a corner, is a beautiful young lady with the most magnificent pair of lips — wonderfully shaped and gloriously plump— anyone has ever seen.

Her name is Marie. Her eyes are perfectly almond shaped and, even though they lack in color, the sparkle they give off is like the moon in the darkest of skies. Her tanned skin is an elegant combination of silky and smooth, while her hair, ravishingly colored in blonde highlights, rests just below her shoulders. Sitting across from her is her almost equally as beautiful friend, Jennifer. She too has a pair of perfectly shaped eyes but hers are emerald. Her skin is creamy and soft toned, while her hair is a dull and simple black that has been curled.

The two young ladies are too deeply involved in their conversation to even notice Aiden.

"If I had to choose between the two... I think I would have to go with eating a dead roach," Marie states.

"Really? You would rather eat a bug than take it up the—"

Jennifer questions before being cut short.

"Whoa, not so loud." Marie glances around. "But yes, yes I would."

"You're gross. I love you, but you're gross."

Jennifer swiftly takes a sip of her wine. "You know, you live your life way too, what's the word? Disney, yeah that's it, Disney."

"Excuse me? How dare you. I do not live my life too Disney."

"Oh, please."

"I'm telling you. I can have my wild moments."

"No, you can't."

"Yes, I can."

"No, you can't, and I'll gladly explain why."

"Okay, humor me."

"Let's look at the facts. You have never left the country, let alone the state, probably not even the city."

"Once," Marie quickly chimes in.

"You've been dating that same tool Chris for over nine months now, whom you'll probably end up marrying because, screw it, why not? Quite frankly, not once have you ever told me anything freaky he's done, in a good way. Nor have you ever come to me with an exciting story about him." Jennifer takes a breath. "I'm just worried you'll end up bringing me little nieces and nephews all prepped out with lifeless bodies."

Marie just glares at her friend before she takes a large mouthful of red wine.

"It's not going to be like that, Jen," Marie says.

"Listen, don't get me wrong, he's a nice guy, but you're so beautiful and have so much to offer. I don't want you looking back wondering what if, while throwing back some dead roaches," Jennifer replies.

"Well, he's very charming."

"Charming? The man looks like Mr Potato Head with glasses."

"Who looks like Mr Potato Head with glasses?" Aiden asks, now standing by the table.

Marie and Jennifer jolt their heads in his direction. There they find the handsome and rugged Aiden smiling his perfect smile down at them.

"Good evening, ladies," he adds while both women just stare aimlessly into his opulent eyes. "I'm just curious as to who looks like Mr Potato Head."

"No one. No one looks like Mr Potato Head," Jennifer says, struggling to gather her words. "It's just my friend, Marie here, thinks guys that look like Mr Potato Head are hot."

"Marie. What a beautiful name. I love that name," Aiden says. "It's funny, Marie, because I think that you're hot."

"Wow! That was just, well, very straightforward of you," Marie replies.

"I call them like I see them."

"Wait, are you even old enough to be in a bar?"

Aiden just laughs, squints his eyes and asks, "What the… are you a cop or something?"

"Detective, actually," Marie responds.

"Well, that's new. I'm twenty-seven, actually."

"You look like you're nineteen with a five o'clock shadow."

"I get that a lot, actually."

"Well Mister Twenty-seven, aren't you too old to be trying to use pickup lines like that with me?"

"If I say no, are you going to shoot me?"

"I'm thinking about it."

Unsure of how serious Marie is, Aiden laughs along with Jennifer. By this time, he usually comes up with something witty to say to sweep the girl off her feet, but for some reason this time seems different. Marie's allure is something he's never come across before. Not even with Skylar. He starts to feel the sweat trickle down his back as the lights from above beam down upon him like rays from a summer day. He feels his palms getting moist and clammy. On a brief mission to hide his nerves, Aiden slowly shoves his hands into his pant pockets.

"You know, Marie, I could ask you if it hurt when you fell from heaven, but I'm sure you already know that line." Aiden pauses. "Truth be told, I haven't been able to take my eyes off you since you got here."

Now Marie's hands start to feel a bit damp. She can feel her underarms get pasty while the wine she drinks keeps hitting the knot stuck in her throat. She can usually ignore any guy that walks over to her, but tonight is not one of those times.

"I'm not going to lie to you, there are a lot of pretty ladies in here tonight, your friend included." Aiden stops and reaches out his hand to greet Jennifer.

"Hi, I'm Aiden. What's your name?"

"I'm... I'm... Jen, I'm Jen," she says dazedly.

"You're very pretty, Jen."

"Have my babies," Jennifer adds slyly.

Looking away from Jennifer, Aiden does a double take back in her direction. It takes him a moment to catch what she said. He softly smirks and then turns back to Marie.

"But there's something different about you. Fact is, I know, without a shadow of doubt, you are the most beautiful woman I have ever had the privilege to lay my eyes on. And please note, Miss Officer, that's not a line whatsoever. That's the truth," says

Aiden. "So, I have to ask, is there a chance you feel the same way?"

Marie's eyes just shoot open. Everything she just heard is simply ravishing and poetic. She can easily tell that Aiden's words are pure and honest. She didn't believe that someone could be so raw and truthful. It's clear to everyone that she is blown away by these words just by her expression.

"She does," Jennifer replies for Marie.

Marie fiercely glares at Jennifer. All she can ponder is why in the world she would say that. She knows Marie is dating someone, even if Aiden is the heart-stopping-attractive kind of guy.

"I don't," Marie finally spits out.

"Does she?" Aiden asks Jennifer.

"Heck yeah she does," she replies while nodding her head.

"Would you cut that out?" Marie asks Jennifer before turning back to Aiden. "I don't."

"She says you do." Aiden points back to Jennifer.

"But I don't."

"But you do," Jennifer adds.

"Seriously, Jen?"

"Okay, how about you start by letting me buy you a drink?" Aiden asks.

"How about you start by showing me some identification?" Marie chimes back.

"For real?"

"Little bit."

"Do you mind if I have a seat?"

"Yes."

"No!" Jennifer firmly rebuts.

Marie, once again, gives her friend a stare that could peer

into your soul and beat you from the inside. Aiden smiles and reaches over to a neighborly table and removes a chair as the couple who are sitting there stare up at him in disbelief. He effortlessly spins the chair around and plants himself so that his chest is pushed up against the backrest.

"Let me just make one last point, and if you don't agree, I'll go. Deal?" asks Aiden.

Marie takes a heavy breath and releases a huff in agreement.

"You and I can both agree that we live in a destructive world that, let's face it, probably doesn't have much time left in it," he says.

"That sounds about right," she responds unsurely.

"With that being said, I have no clue how much longer I'll be on this planet, and I'm sure you have no clue as to how long you're going to be here."

"If you don't get to the point, I'm going to know exactly how long you'll be here after I put a bullet inside you."

"All right, all right. All I'm trying to say is there will never be a day in your life that you'll look back and say, 'Damn, that Aiden guy really sucked in bed.' But you will think to yourself that you should've found out."

"Wow. You're incredible," she says, surprised at what she just heard.

"No, you're incredible."

Aiden stops for a second and realizes all the nonsense that just spewed from his mind and through his mouth. Even he is amazed at its ludicrousness. He's been a lot of things, but at a loss of words isn't one of them. All the while, Jennifer enjoys every moment of this conversation.

"Okay, restart. May I please get you ladies a round?" he politely suggests.

Dumbfounded, Marie removes her leather coat from the back of her chair and wraps it around her perfectly sleek and tender neck, draping the sides over her gorgeous strapless magenta top.

"Okay. I think it's time that we go before my trigger finger starts to itch," Marie replies.

"We? As in me and you?" Aiden asks, smiling.

"Well, what do you know, there goes that finger."

"I'll tell the valet to bring my car around. Or maybe we should take yours? Probably yours, huh? On the count I've probably had more drinks than you tonight."

Marie springs up from her chair, reaches over the table and grabs hold of Jennifer's arm. She gently tugs on it like a puppy on a newspaper just before uttering the words, "Let's go."

Marie scurries off with her best friend in hand, whose eyes refuse to let Aiden out of her sight.

"Good night!" Aiden shouts.

Neither of his former guests reply. Instead, all he receives is a blown kiss by Jennifer as she waves farewell while being dragged outside. Aiden can't help but laugh, knowing that image will most likely stay with him for at least the next month or two. He then stands up and securely places the chair he was just sitting on back at the table he took it from. He then locks eyes with Kenneth, who seemingly has been watching the whole event transpire. He quickly walks over to the bar and finds himself back at the side of his best friend.

"So, how'd it go?" Kenneth asks with a deep grin.

"I'd say it went as well as expected," Aiden answers, hopping back on top of his bar stool.

"That bad, huh?"

"It could've been a lot worse, in my opinion. But I was right.

It was too soon."

"I don't think it was too soon, my friend. I just think you've been out of the game for far too long."

Aiden chuckles. "And what would you know about the game, sir?"

"Clearly more than you at this point."

The two friends share a good laugh, a much-needed laugh.

"Well, if nothing else pops up, you can come over and cuddle with me tonight," Kenneth adds.

"I don't think I am drunk enough for that just yet."

"Say no more." He pauses. "Bartender, can you bring us another round and a shot of your finest tequila for my friend here?"

"Let me rephrase that Ken: I'll never be drunk enough for that." He laughs even louder.

"We shall see about that."

Once more, the friends laugh together and say their cheers to the night. Aiden will be forever thankful for his friendship with Kenneth. But as they enjoy their beverages together, Aiden takes one last look towards the entrance and smiles to himself. He can't help but wonder if he will ever cross paths with Marie again. The thought of this being more than just some coincidence races through his mind over and over. A loud thought circles in his mind that this meeting was supposed to happen. This meeting was the beginning of the world, brand new.

Act I
Chapter 3
Start the Day, Just to Close the Curtains

The day is bright and new. A small gleam of light makes its way through a small opening of the large blinds hanging from a window nearby. The light, belonging to the sun's rays, beams down on Aiden's glistening back, causing small pellets of sweat to slide into the bed sheets below. The rest of the room is engulfed in darkness, making any pathway impossible to find. It's the way Aiden loves to sleep, especially after a drunken night.

Off in the distance, a loud banging echoes throughout the dimly lit room. Aiden barely makes a move, but the banging grows louder and more frequent. While it continues to grow, Aiden finally begins to stir. Once more the banging progresses until Aiden can no longer ignore it. As his eyes finally open slowly, he lets out a subtle groan. Suddenly, the pounding stops, making Aiden believe that the booms he heard were just in his dream. He begins to trust his thoughts when a stable vibration commences off to the right of his bed. With his eyes once again closed, he gradually reaches out his right arm and lifts his phone from the dresser.

Aiden places the phone to his ear and is only able to muster a moan of displeasure.

"Open your damn door already," a voice replies to Aiden's moan.

Aiden moans once more.

"NOW!" the voice says while another thud bounces off the

front door.

"All right already," Aiden says.

In one quick swoop, Aiden tosses his bed sheet aside, revealing his nude body. Trying to fight the struggle between his body and brain, he lazily slides his legs off the side of the bed. Waiting just below the brass frame of his bed is a pair of charcoal-colored sweatpants. With close to little effort, Aiden snatches his pants off the ground and slides each leg in simultaneously. With a few huffs and puffs, he rubs his eyes desperately. Finally, with all the strength he has, he pushes off the mattress and heads towards the bedroom door. With no struggle at all, Aiden swings open the door, steps through the archway and into his even darker living room.

Upon his first step, Aiden roughly smacks his foot against something. The sound of the thud booms throughout the shadows.

"Mother fu—" he lets out while closing his bedroom door.

Instead of finishing his distasteful comment, Aiden just hisses while hearing an additional tap against his front door. This time it's much gentler, like that of a ticking clock.

"I'm coming. Relax," Aiden responds to the tap.

Without dawdling, Aiden swiftly reaches the door, unlatches the chain just above eye level and unlocks the doorknob. He hesitantly opens the door, causing the sunlight to forcibly barge in. Aiden is then greeted by a loving ear-to-ear grin.

"Good morning, honey," Kenneth says with two large cups in hand.

"What on earth are you doing here, Kenneth?" Aiden responds.

"Now is that anyway to greet your lover?"

"I'm not your lover."

"Whatever. Just let me in." He pauses. "I come bearing gifts. And no, don't worry, it's not another baby."

Kenneth raises the cups up to Aiden's eyes just before pushing his way into the apartment. The door closes and the ceiling light illuminates.

"Whoa!" Kenneth spews out.

Kenneth takes a look around Aiden's living room and sees nothing but dullness. The walls are plain and bare like a newborn. In the middle of the room lies a single and sad-looking beige leather couch. The carpet below is a musty grey and to Kenneth's belief is only worthy of holding a dozen half-opened cardboard boxes. The one eye-popping thing about the room is the overly large television leaning against the back wall because it does not have a proper TV stand.

"I see we still haven't managed to fully move in," Kenneth says.

"Less talkie, more coffee," Aiden replies stepping towards his friend and then removing one of the cups from his grasp.

"Dude, what did I say about being shirtless around me? If you want me to stop being gay for you, you gotta cover that up," he adds jokingly, pointing to Aiden's shirtless torso.

Kenneth begins to just stare at Aiden's bulging muscles while sipping on his coffee. It's as if Aiden were carved from stone and belonged in a museum somewhere, posing for strangers to gawk at.

"Dude!" Aiden exclaims while leaning back on the sofa.

"What? What?" Kenneth mumbles.

"My eyes are up here."

"Sorry, damn. Who told you to be a walking photoshop model?"

"Yeah, yeah. Whatever you say." Aiden takes a quick gulp

of coffee. "So, what are you doing here?"

"You know you shouldn't down your coffee like that."

"Dude!"

"Okay, okay. No but seriously, you shouldn't…"

In two big steps, Aiden places his hand on the knob.

"All right, time to go," Aiden adds pretending to open the door to kick his friend out.

"Fine, I'll stop," Kenneth replies.

"Thank you. Now, why are you here?"

"I don't know. It's a beautiful day out. I thought I'd stop by and see what my best friend is up to."

"Kenneth?"

"Yes?"

"Don't bullshit me."

Kenneth shrugs his shoulders and looks over to his best friend with such concern. The wrinkles on his forehead start to coincide with his hairline. His overly warming grin fuses into a frown of hopelessness. He slowly moves back and is now in the position Aiden was previously in.

"I haven't forgotten what day it is today, Aiden. I've held this day near and dear to my heart, just as you have. I just thought that maybe this year, this one year, you'd let me in, and we can finally visit—"

"No." Aiden quickly shuts his friend down.

"Aiden. Come on, man."

"No."

Kenneth is a strong man, but he has never been strong enough to hold back emotions from Aiden when he pushes him away. Kenneth's eyes instantly fill with water, making them almost glass-like. His eyelids begin to swell while the balls hurriedly change from a glowing white to a lifeless pink. Aiden notices and rushes back to his friend's side. He follows along with Kenneth and presses the lower part of his back against the couch. He then wraps his bulky arm around Kenneth and brings him in tight in comfort.

"I understand what you are trying to do, I really do. But this year is not the year. No year will ever be the year, Ken. I'm sorry," Aiden says.

Kenneth lets out a small whimper and quickly brushes it away.

"I just don't want you to be alone. Not any more. Not today."

"I'm not alone."

Kenneth calmly wipes away the tears from his face like a child who has just recovered from an injury. He then wraps one arm around Aiden's back before using the other hand to sweep the tears off his friend's abdominal muscles. He makes sure to take his time on each protruding muscle before uttering, "You know what would make me really happy right now?"

"No, Kenneth. I'm not gay!"

Both men quickly let go of each other and share a smile.

"Oh, come on. How would you know unless you try it?"

"I know I'm not. But I promise, if I ever change my mind, you'll be the first to know."

"Promise?"

"I swear."

Kenneth awkwardly raises his hand waiting for Aiden to give him a high five. Aiden just shakes his head in amusement and indulges his buddy. Kenneth's infectious smile returns to his face, followed by a double fist pump to show his excitement.

"So, how's about we unpack all this crap already?" Kenneth asks.

"How's about we enjoy the rest of these coffees together and then you go on your merry way?" Aiden says, shutting him down.

"Seriously?"

"This doesn't change anything. I still want to go through this day as I do every year, by myself, possibly with a bottle or two and some very, very loud music."

Kenneth snickers and nods his head in agreement. He then lifts himself off the back of the couch and walks around to sit on the soft yet worn out cushions. Aiden, on the other hand, throws himself backwards and rolls to his feet just before jumping onto the couch, butt first. He takes another look at his best friend and simply smiles. With just one look, Kenneth knows that this smile means nothing at all. It's broken and so is the story Aiden's eyes are telling. He's the only man that knows Aiden better than Aiden probably knows himself. He also knows Aiden is as stubborn as he is attractive, and to Kenneth he is "movie star" good looking. So, instead of persisting and starting an unnecessary fight, he just smiles back, lifts his cup and says, "Cheers."

"Cheers, my old friend," Aiden says, pressing his cup alongside Kenneth's.

Suddenly, in the distance, a squeaking sound scratches against Aiden and Kenneth's ear drums. Synchronically, both men turn their attention to the back of the room and find a beautiful, long-legged bombshell of a woman exiting Aiden's bedroom. Her hair is a fiery red that is greatly compensated by her pale, Snow White-like complexion. Her eyes are a piercing green that would make any man melt.

Noticing that she is now under the attention of two pairs of eyes, her cheeks begin to fill with a color like that of a freshly bloomed rose. She rapidly makes her way past the men sitting just a few feet away from her. They refuse to unlock their sights from her. Just before unlocking the front door, she looks back at

Aiden and smiles the most gracious of smiles.

"Last night was amazing, Aiden."

"It sure was," he responds with uncertainty.

"I left my number on your dresser, by the way. Feel free to use it as you please."

Aiden just stares, unable to form any sentence. Kenneth sees the hopeless look on his friend's face and giggles as he smacks the side of Aiden's arm. Aiden furiously looks at Kenneth, realizing he just did that to get his attention. Kenneth nods his head and mouths the words, "Let her out."

"Right," Aiden says aloud, springing to his feet.

He rushes over to this woman's side and utters the words, "Let me get that for you."

"Why, thank you sir," she says, still blushing.

Aiden gently opens the door, allowing the young woman out. Just as she is about to exit, she gently jerks her head towards Aiden. He in turn does the same maneuver, forcing them into the most awkward kiss goodbye anyone has ever seen — especially for Kenneth, because his only reaction is to slap his forehead and burst out in laughter.

"Well, have a great day. Don't forget to call me," she adds before stepping out onto the front balcony.

"I won't. I'll be seeing you," Aiden adds.

Aiden softly closes the door. As he feels the vibration of the locks locking in his arms, Aiden turns around hesitantly. He knows his friend's judgmental expressions are awaiting him, ready to pounce like a tigress. With no real option, he unhurriedly turns himself around and is greeted with a wide-eyed Kenneth with a smile to match.

"Dude!" Kenneth pauses. "Who the hell was that?"

"That? That was… That's…"

"You don't even remember her name?"

"Of course, I... don't."

Unable to hold back their composure, the friends explode with laughter. Their once sorrowful expressions have vanished and are replaced with much needed enjoyment. The two indulge in the amusement. Aiden grips his sides due to the welcoming pain from laughing too much.

"You know, for a supposed straight man, that was one gay-ass kiss goodbye," Kenneth claims.

"Shut up!" Aiden barely utters through the cracks of laughter.

Now sitting side by side again, Aiden just looks at his best friend in amazement. He can't help but wonder how he ended up with such a loving and amazing best friend like the one he has. Though he is going to stick to his guns and spend the rest of the day alone, he appreciates this moment. Deep down, he's truly gracious to share a moment like this, no matter how short lived it will be. His friendship with Kenneth means the world to him and even though he's ready to shut out the world, it's the one thing that'll get him through the hours.

Act I
Chapter 4
Imagine a Time the Truth Ran Free

Around the same time that Aiden is enjoying his sweetened coffee, Marie is sitting across town at her favorite restaurant. She is surrounded by her boyfriend, a few co-workers and of course, her best friend, Jennifer. Together they share a few drinks, a delicious meal and some kind words. Among them is a close to crowded scene, with mixture of different conversations blended horribly together.

Marie, sitting thigh-to-thigh with Jennifer, is fully engaged in a conversation with her friend until the sound of metal viciously clanging up against glass rumbles around their table.

"Pardon me, guys. If you'd just indulge me for a brief moment," a man says, now standing among his peers.

The man is quite tall, slender and dressed in a suit that is one size too large. On his face rests a pair of thin-framed glasses that don't really go well with his strong, yet somehow, chubby cheeks. Just under those is a bulbous and very noticeable-sized nose that looks as though it may be able to smell every single dish that surrounds him. This nose does no justice to the thick and bushy mustache that lies beneath it. Yet, the most notable feature of this man is his thin, almost invisible kisser. His name is Christopher, and he is the man that has been dating Marie for the better part of a year.

"I would like to give a small speech in honor of my lovely lady here. I'm talking about Marie, of course," Christopher adds.

The group looks on with smiles and chuckles at what was an attempt to be a joke. Jennifer, who doesn't fancy Christopher, follows up with a very faint and very fake laugh.

"First, let me just say thank you all for joining us today," he adds. "Second, to my spicy momma…"

Christopher pauses waiting for laughter, which he quickly receives from everyone except Jennifer, who just rolls her eyes.

"I'd like to be the first to congratulate you on your most recent promotion to detective," Christopher continues. "And even though all the T's have not been crossed and the I's have not been dotted, I just know in my heart of hearts, you're going to be the most amazing female detective this city has ever seen."

Christopher takes a quick glimpse around the table with eyes full of tears before uttering his conclusion.

"On that note, I salute you, fair lady." He raises his glass. "To Marie!"

"To Marie!" everyone responds with their glasses lifted as well.

Everyone shoves their drinks into their faces and slowly sips. Meanwhile, Christopher takes a few steps around, places himself next to Jennifer and leans over so that both she and Marie are at eye level with him.

"Okay, so here's the deal, ladies. I know Miss Detective here isn't official just yet," Christopher says.

"So you've mentioned," Jennifer replies annoyed.

"Right. With that being said, when she does become official, we are going to go ahead and throw her a second party with all of her friends and loved ones, right here at this very same location."

"Okay?"

"I'm just telling you because you're the very first invitee, and I truly hope you can make it, because I promise it'll be a night to remember."

"You got it, dude."

"Good. Glad to hear it."

Before walking away and joining the rest of his comrades, Christopher leans in and plants the most innocent of kisses onto Marie's forehead, like that of an overprotective father. Watching, Jennifer rolls her eyes and shakes her head in sickness. She patiently waits for him to walk away as she releases a strong, "Oh God!"

Not able to understand what she is so disgusted by, Marie turns to her friend and questions, "What? What's wrong now?"

"Were you not paying attention?"

"What exactly should I have paid attention to here?"

"Um. His not very subtle remark about a night to remember."

"Okay, what of it?"

"Oh, my gosh. If you didn't catch on, you're blinder than he is."

"What is it?"

"Marie. He's totally going to propose."

'What? No... No... He's not, he wouldn't."

"Oh, please. He has it written all over his face."

"You think so?"

Marie's expression changes from questionable to slightly intrigued by the suggestion. She then looks over to Christopher and releases a nervous giggle.

"Oh, no," Jennifer spews. "Don't tell me you want him to?"

"I don't know. Maybe. He's very sweet and caring."

"Marie, sweetie, you can't be serious."

"I'm just saying."

"When was the last time you looked at yourself? Like, truly

looked at yourself? You're a filet mignon and he's, I don't know, French fries."

"Oh, stop."

"It's true. And if you end up with French fries, please tell me what on earth do I end up with?"

Marie's eyes begin to get squint as she glares at her best friend with a side grin. Though she can see where Jennifer is coming from, she keeps telling herself that it's not all about his looks, but what he brings to her happiness.

"He's not really that bad, Jen, you know it."

"Fine, fine. I'm not going to shame you or guilt you out of it," Jennifer replies while she takes another glance at Christopher.

Still not able to see what in the world Marie sees in the man, Jennifer just shakes her head and asks, "Jesus! Are you sure? I mean, look at him. On top of that, I am your only friend here. Everyone else is a stuffed tool in a suit that only came because of him. Do you really want to be surrounded by that forever?"

"Jen!"

"Okay, fine. I get the hint. I shall no longer speak on the matter. You're free to do what you want."

"Thank you."

After her statement, Jennifer jumps out of her seat and pushes it forward forcefully. She picks up her pocketbook that is hanging just to the side of her chair, aggressively reaches in and removes cash that she then places on the table. The cash gently flutters down while her coins come crashing down, causing a noticeable ruckus.

"On that note, it's time for me to get out of here," Jennifer adds while leaning in and kissing Marie's cheek. "Enjoy the rest of the day, love."

"Thank you. Call me later," Marie says.

"You got it." Jennifer pauses. "See you later, everyone."

Jennifer receives no verbal responses. Instead, she gets a bunch of hands up in the air waving her off as everyone continues on in their conversation. She just shrugs, tilts her head to the sky and raises her arms in disbelief whilst staring in Marie's direction, suggesting that they can't be serious. Marie just brushes her friend off with a blown kiss goodbye.

While her best friend finally exits, Marie looks on to the crowd she has been left with. She takes a real, deep glance over at her boyfriend and tries to picture a life with him. She attempts to think of the future they might have together, but all she can see up to is the proposal and nothing more. Suddenly, thoughts of the night before strike in her memory. She questions whether this is the man for her.

Her visions of a proposal then turn into daydreams of her in an exquisite white gown, with her trotting down a lovely flower-filled garden. In the far distance, a well-tailored man awaits her arrival. She patiently waits for his head to turn. When it finally does, she's shocked to find it's not the face of her mustached boyfriend but the face belonging to the man she met less than twenty-four hours ago. It's Aiden. But why Aiden, she questions. More conflicted than ever, Marie just shrugs it to the side and tries one last time to picture her wedding with the man she's with now. But no matter how hard she tries, she just can't. She's had way crazier thoughts than this one, but for some reason, it just doesn't seem to be all that crazy.

Act I
Chapter 5
All the Mistakes One Life Can Take

The bright afternoon has now become a somber twilight. A clock, off in the distance, illuminates 10.18 p.m. in a lightless room. The echoes of old pipes and drains bounce from one wall to the next. The sounds of vicious dogs barking linger in the background. Suddenly, there's a faint tapping of bone against wood. It goes off on a steady three-point beat. It stops. After just a moment, it returns but this time with a little more strength and speed added to it. It comes to a halt once more. Just then, the dusky room is filled with dim lighting. Though there's not much light, it reveals faintly nauseating green painted walls. Walls that seem very worn out but are decorated with wooden picture frames and burnished awards.

Feet trampling downstairs overpower clanging pipes. For a final time, the point knock is heard, but this time it's greeted by a soft, yet stern, voice.

"I'm coming. I'm coming," a man calls out.

Gowned in a navy-blue robe, the old gentleman quickly wraps himself up to conceal his lackluster pajama pants. Reaching the bottom of the stairway, he slides into a pair of old slippers that are torn at the seams and unveil pieces of cotton spilling out like guts from a corpse. Now, with feet covered, the man gently glides his feet against the hard floor below him until he reaches his home's front door. He swiftly undoes his locks just before slowly opening the door to see who his uninvited guest is.

There he sees a young man dressed in plain jeans, a black buttoned-down top and a pair of old school basketball sneakers.

"Aiden?" he says with much surprise while fully swinging the door open.

Now toe-to-toe with the man, Aiden rests his back against the brick frame just inches away and gives a toothy grin.

"Sheesh, Aiden. What are you doing here?"

"In honor of today's special event, I thought I'd stop by. Maybe catch up and have a beer with my pops," Aiden replies, now standing upright.

He kindly raises his arm just above eye level, revealing a six-pack of beer. The man steps a little closer, fully revealing his face.

Aiden is almost identical to his father, Hal. The only differences are Hal's much stronger and squared jawline, the slightly larger bridge of the nose and some salt added to his hair.

"It looks like you've already started without me," Hal says.

"Yeah, well... you know."

For just a moment, both men stare at each other in an uncomfortable silence. Thinking rather smoothly, Aiden subtly notices his father's ample and bulky physique.

"You're looking good, dad. Back to the gym, I see," Aiden comments.

"Yeah. I'm trying at least. Can't let age stop me now," Hal responds.

"The main man, Hal. We always said you'd outlive us all."

Hal just looks at his son in disbelief. His eyes begin to shine as he smiles at his boy. It's been many years since he's seen Aiden, and even though it's unexpected, it's still a wonderful surprise.

Aiden quickly cuts off his father's precious moment by pushing the bottles of beer he brought up against Hal's chest.

"Like I was going to say, I come bearing gifts. Gifts I'm sure we can both use," Aiden adds.

Hal's loving vision of his son quickly vanishes and turns to remorse. He looks on in pity with his soft, puppy dog eyes.

"I'm sorry, Aiden. I don't drink that any more," Hal says with sympathy.

With a face full of confusion, Aiden looks down at the beers and asks, "Wait, what do you mean? Did you start drinking different stuff?"

"No," Hal pauses. "How about you come inside, and we can talk. How's that sound?"

Aiden squints with great confusion expressed on his face.

"Come in, come in."

Hal gently grips onto his son's shoulder and guides Aiden into his home. Aiden walks in, forcefully freeing himself from his father's grip and proceeds into the equally dull painted living room. With no television in sight, the only things to welcome him are a set of outdated leather couches, a matching torn up love seat and an, unnecessary shrine to Aiden's childhood and teenage years. From pictures of his first bath to his first little league baseball game, all the way up to his senior prom. Even though they may have stopped talking, Hal makes it clear that he is still very proud of his boy, viewing him as some sort of saint to worship.

Aiden walks over to a large bookshelf where most of his sports trophies and awards from school rest. Just beside it is a small marble countertop where Hal's house phone sits. Aiden gently pushes it over, deciding that's a good place to put his beers. He then snatches a bottle out of the case and walks over to his father's old, and decrepit, fireplace. Above it is an additional countertop where more pictures of Aiden's adolescent years are.

Pictures of memories that Aiden hasn't thought about in quite some time.

With the front door closed behind him, Hal wanders off from behind Aiden and into the back area where his kitchen is.

"I'll make us some tea," Hal calls back.

"I really like what you've done with the place," Aiden replies while still looking around.

"I haven't changed anything, Aiden."

"Exactly."

"Well, I never saw a reason to fix anything. Like the old saying goes... if it isn't broken, don't fix it."

"I'm surprised you didn't have some woman move in and remodel this place."

"Well... after everything we went through, I figured, why bother?"

Now entering the living room with two mugs in hand, Hal cautiously walks over to his son. He politely nudges Aiden with his elbow, offering the cup.

"Oh... you were serious about the tea? I thought it was your way of being modest," Aiden says.

"Nope. I'm very serious when it comes to teatime," Hal responds.

"Teatime?" Aiden asks with confusion spreading across his face. "Man, we haven't spoken in ten years, and you want to have tea?"

"I don't drink that stuff any more, son. I've been sober..." Hal takes a moment to ponder, "... for about five years now."

Aiden is taken aback and expresses this very vividly. He stares into his father's eyes and smiles a smile full of sarcasm.

"Come on. We didn't get to celebrate my big twenty-one. Never even shared our first beer together. Have one with me,"

Aiden insists.

Aiden reaches back and grabs a second bottle, offering it to his father. Hal, once again, kindly refuses. Noticing his father is serious about not drinking, Aiden's expression switches from a cheesy smile to an annoyed grin.

"Fine. More for me," Aiden says, placing the second bottle back in its place.

Aiden then pops the top off his original beer and tosses the cap carelessly to the ground before taking a gigantic gulp. Hal is oblivious to his son's actions, as he has already turned away and is slowly sliding into his love seat. Aiden turns back around and resumes looking at the photos that rest above the fireplace. After a moment's passing, he comes across one that really catches his attention. In the far-right corner, he finds an old snapshot of himself on his graduation day. He remembers it so well because in the picture he wore his grandfather's favorite tie in order to honor him since he had passed away just a few months before.

Though that tie meant so much to him, that's not what he loves most about that moment. Just to his left in the photo is his mother. Gowned in a lovely yellow summer dress, she has her arms wrapped around his waist with the most marvelous smile. It was so rare to find a picture without her smiling in it. Aiden's eyes tend to just fixate on his strong, yet gorgeous, mother. Her hair done in waves and slightly pinned back. Her makeup, which she hardly ever wore, seemed so perfect that it would have you think a professional did it.

Aiden hesitantly reaches out for the frame as his hand begins to tremble. He carefully removes it from its place of rest and brings it close to his chest. Now, looking down upon it, he places his right hand on where his mother is standing and gently caresses it, as if he is trying to feel his mother through the glass.

Without notice, a tear falls from Aiden's face and splatters on the glass.

"That was one of her proudest moments, Aiden," Hal says.

Aiden promptly reacts to the sound of his father's voice by wiping away any proof of emotion.

"Yeah? Well, that's not what I remember about that day," Aiden replies with a sniffle.

"No? So, what is it that you remember about that day?"

"I remember wondering where you were. Wondering if you were going to show up for once," he adds while placing the photo back in its place of setting. "I remember thinking to myself, it's just like any other day... why would he bother to show?"

Aiden leisurely turns to his father, whose eyes are locked onto his son.

"Funny thing is, she tried covering for you. Said you were stuck at work and that your boss refused to let you leave. But I knew... I knew the truth."

"Aiden, I—" Hal attempts to speak.

"I knew you were off at some bar, drinking your life away, just like any... other... day!"

Hal just sits in his chair, filled with nothing but despair and regret. He looks at his son with hopelessness. He can feel an enormous ball begin to build in is throat that seems to be keeping him from saying all the right things or, maybe in Aiden's mind, all the wrong things.

"I know why you came here, son." Hal chokes up.

"You know why I'm here?" Aiden responds angrily.

"Yes."

"Please, enlighten me," Aiden adds.

Aiden stumbles over to the couch just across from where his father has a seat. He proceeds to chug down what's almost half the bottle of beer while awaiting his father's response.

"Today is her anniversary. The day she was taken from us," Hal says with remorse.

"From us?" Aiden exclaims. "Us? There was no us! She was taken from me!"

"Aiden..."

"No... No! Don't you dare sit there and claim to have had any ounce of care. You know damn well it was your fault."

Hal has a fully formed ball in his throat. Every word that he tries to spit out refuses to come out. It's as though they just bounce off and shoot down into his chest. It is at this point he is unable to look Aiden in the eyes and his head collapses from the weight on his shoulders.

"I'm sorry, son," Hal finally manages to get out.

"Sorry?" Aiden snarls. "Your sorry is ten years too late."

"You know, I tried finding you when I got sober," Hal adds, looking up at his son.

"Oh, so you were going to settle with being five years too late. Good job, Hal."

"Hal? I'm Hal now?"

"You know, it's funny. It's taken me ten years to realize this." Aiden pauses. "It wasn't only my mother who died that night, but my father as well."

With those words, Hal's heart shatters. Tears begin to consume his face as his son watches on. He drops his head once more, feeling deep inside that he is truly unworthy of Aiden's love and forgiveness. Wanting to cause further heartache, Aiden looks on and adds, "So yes, from here on out, you're just some guy named Hal."

Aiden then takes an additional look around the room, focusing in on each and every picture of himself.

"You should really get rid of all this shit," Aiden says. "It's like some kind of sick shrine to your dead son."

Hal refuses to acknowledge Aiden's hurtful suggestion. His lips start to quiver, and his hands begin to rattle. It's taking all of his composure to not burst out weeping in front of his son.

"Who knew that one day I would like you more if you were drunk? It's crazy what old memories will reveal to you, huh, Hal?"

Aiden gently leans into the cushions surrounding him and kindly rests his head. His eyes gradually close from exhaustion. Hal just watches on. For the first time tonight, there is a sense of calmness to the world. The dogs, once howling at one another, have ceased. The pipes have quit their tinkering. And Aiden's harsh words have stopped flowing. With all that in mind, Hal looks on at his drunken son, who is now hunched over with beer still in hand. For him, what seems like a precious moment will only ever be a horrid nightmare.

No longer able to hold his composure, Hal releases an ugly, yet powerful, cry. Afraid he may wake his raging beast of a son, he rapidly grabs a pillow from behind his back and roughly pounds his face into it. His sobs do their best to escape but are greatly muffled. Hal fully engulfs the pillow, wrapping his arms completely around it. Giving all his might, he squeezes the cushion while praying to himself to wake up, but he knows this is no dream. This is an endless night he knew would make its way to him somehow. And now that it is finally here, Hal wishes it had never come.

Act II
Chapter 6
Sorry, Daughter, But Your Father's Not the Same

It has been two weeks since Aiden was face-to-face with his father. Two weeks since he let out all his pent-up frustration for his father that he has held in for the past ten years. But on this day, Aiden finds himself with yet another one of his family members. Today Aiden sits in an old but well-furnished booth at one of his favorite diners. The seats are very soft, bouncy, and draped in red. In front of him is a half-eaten plate of pancakes, drenched in syrup. Sitting on the other side of the table, also with a half-eaten plate of pancakes is his daughter, Marie. Her face, though very pale, is filled with light and love as she stuffs another piece of pancake in her already cluttered mouth.

Aiden just sits in silence as he watches Marie shovel food into her mouth, fork free.

"You know, you can use your spoon or fork to eat, baby," Aiden says.

"I know, daddy," Marie replies with particles of food splattering from her grin.

"Well... as long as you know."

Aiden then glances just above Marie's head and notices a clock. Its hand draws closer and closer to twelve o'clock.

"It's almost time to go, Marie," Aiden adds.

"Go where?" Marie questions.

"Home."

"Are we going to your house, daddy?"

"No, baby. Daddy is going to go to his house and you're going to go with mommy."

"But why can't I go with you?"

"Because that's not how this works."

"Why not?"

"Because that's how the judge said it has to be."

"What does that mean, daddy?"

"I'll explain it to you one day. For now, just finish your food."

"Okay, daddy."

Aiden's eyes quickly shoot back towards the clock. He knows there's not much time left. Over in the corner, a man slowly rises to his feet. He's a rather heavy-set man with a thick, yet tidy, mustache. He reaches in his back pocket, pulls out his wallet and places some money on the counter before him. He then looks in Aiden's direction, pointing him out to one of the waitresses. He places the wallet back into his pocket, grabs a pair of jackets and walks over to Aiden and Marie.

"Miss Marie… ready to go?" The man asks, handing Marie her jean jacket.

"Do we have to?" she asks, sucking her teeth.

"I'm sorry sweetie, but yeah, we have to."

"Okay."

Marie slides out of her end of the booth, placing both feet on the ground. She goes to reach for her jacket but is interrupted by her father's words.

"Maybe you should wipe your hands first, baby," Aiden says, handing her a pair of napkins.

"Thank you, daddy," she replies, retrieving the napkins from her father.

Marie then roughly rubs her hands against one another with

the cloth sandwiched between them. Aiden just watches on in amusement. To everyone else, cleaning their hands is just an everyday thing, but for him to watch his daughter do it in such a manner makes him think it is one of the cutest things he has ever seen. While Aiden smiles, watching his daughter, Marie is finally ready to put her jacket on. Aiden then removes himself from his seat and stands by his daughter's side. He gestures to the man for the jacket and receives it with no contest. He lowers himself to one knee, now placing himself at eye level with Marie as he attempts to cover her up.

"I can do it, daddy. I know how," Marie claims, stopping her father.

"I know you know how. But sometimes it's okay to let daddy help you," Aiden replies with a large grin.

"Ugh... fine. You can help me, but next time I want to do it by myself."

"You got it, kid."

Aiden holds the jacket open while Marie places her arms in very slowly, one at a time. And as soon as the cuffs hit her delicate wrists, Aiden spins his daughter around and is greeted with her warm and mousy giggle.

"Again, daddy! Again!" Marie demands.

"Again? I think once is good enough," he responds with a laugh of his own.

"Oh, come on..."

"Next time, baby. I don't want to do it too much with that full belly of yours," he adds, gently tickling her stomach. "But I want you to know that I had an amazing time with you today."

"So did I."

"I am glad to hear it. Now come give your old man a hug."

"You are not old, daddy."

"I know, I know. It's just a saying, baby."

Aiden lunges his arms out, indicating to his daughter it is time to say goodbye. Marie quickly embraces him with what she thinks is a tight squeeze. He too places her in a hold, but his is much gentler.

"This is my big bear hug, daddy," Marie whispers in Aiden's ear.

"But we aren't bears," Aiden replies.

"I know, I know. It's just a saying, daddy," she says, pushing back off her father's shoulders.

Aiden looks on in amazement just before releasing a love-filled laugh, noticing his daughter just used his same words on him.

"You're too smart for your own good, you know that, little girl?"

"I know."

Aiden, with eyes full of tears, leans in and kisses her forehead before uttering, "I love you, baby."

"I love you too, daddy."

He then roughly clears his throat, slightly shakes his head, and stands back up. He turns to the man and reaches his hand out, gesturing for a peaceful farewell. The man smiles and obliges.

"Thank you, Henry. I really appreciate this," Aiden says.

"Of course. Anything for that little girl," he answers back. "Same time next week?"

"I wouldn't miss it."

Henry now turns his attention to Marie and asks, "Ready to go?"

"Yeah, I'm ready to go," Marie answers.

Marie takes Henry by the hand and the two begin to walk towards the exit. Just before getting to the door, Marie forces

Henry to stop walking, frees herself from his grip and dashes towards Aiden. As she arrives at her father's waist, she leaps into his open arms and immediately hugs him once more. She then follows up with a sweet peck on his cheek and smoothly slides back down onto the ground. She runs back over to Henry's side, grabbing his hand once more.

Just as the two begin to make their exit, Marie turns back to Aiden, waves goodbye and says, "Bye, Daddy. I'll see you later."

Aiden replies, "Bye, baby. Tell Everest I said hi."

"I will!"

The sound of a bell goes off, indicating that Marie has finally left. Aiden greatly fights the urge to burst out in tears while watching his daughter walk away, going past the front window of the diner. Seeing it as the only way not to lose it at that moment, Aiden sits back down in the booth and places his face into his palms. His leg, slightly poking out from under the table, launches into a violent shake. His hands harshly grip onto his face and some of his hair. The sides of his cheeks begin to instantly swell as the blood rushes through.

Just then, a hand is placed on Aiden's back.

"You okay, man?"

Aiden jumps at the touch and slams his hands to his sides. He looks up and is greeted by the wonderful face of Kenneth. He tries to hide his anguish with a grin, but he knows Kenneth sees right through it and removes the smile without a second thought.

"I'm as good as can be, I suppose," says Aiden.

"It's gonna get better, buddy. I promise," Kenneth adds, now sitting where Marie sat just moments ago.

"I've been told."

"Yes, but I actually mean it."

Kenneth reaches out and grabs Aiden's hands, giving them a

gentle tug.

"Hey... I promise things will get better, Aiden."

Aiden looks at his friend with broken eyes, unable to respond. Tears slowly drip down onto his lips, creating a barrier, making the words he wants to say impossible to release.

"Don't... Do. Not. Do. That... If you start crying, then I start crying. And if we are both crying then we look like a bunch of homos in here."

Aiden is able to put his tears on hold and simply glares at Kenneth.

"Yes... I do realize I am an actual homo, but you understand where I am coming from." Kenneth rapidly reaches into his jacket pocket and pulls out a tissue. "Here. Wipe away those nasty tears," he then adds, handing the tissue to Aiden.

Aiden picks the tissue from Kenneth's palm and faintly wipes away his tears.

"Thank you," says Aiden.

"You are very welcome."

"Wait... Did you stay here the whole time?"

"Of course I did. I wouldn't leave my best friend in such a time."

"You didn't have to do that."

"Didn't have to? Dude, what part of BEST FRIEND do you not get?"

Aiden's only response is to smile at the love Kenneth has for him.

"Now then, let's talk about how your date went with that beautiful little girl."

"It went as well as a ninety-minute supervised visit with her grandfather watching could go," Aiden says in disgust.

"Don't focus on the negatives, Aiden. Focus on the fact that you finally get to spend time with that precious angel, who I might add, is looking more and more like you every day."

"She looks like her mother."

"Dude, if you don't stop, I promise I am going to kick the holy hell out of you underneath this table."

"Don't!"

"Then cut the crap already."

Kenneth sees he won't be able to get through to Aiden. At least not right now. Not in this state of mind.

"You know what... We are going out tonight!" Kenneth adds. And just as Aiden is about to give a reason not to, Kenneth quickly cuts him off. "And I'm not taking no for an answer. You literally have no say in the matter. Am I clear?"

"Uh..." Aiden replies but is strongly shut down.

"Am I clear?"

"Fine."

"Fine? No, try again."

"Yes..."

"Yes, what?"

"Dude, shut up."

"I'll take it!"

The two friends share a laugh. A smile returns to the face of Aiden for the first time since his daughter left.

"Now that's what I like to see. That wonderful, heart-melting, Aiden smile," Kenneth says.

"Stop being gay," Aiden responds.

"Never."

Aiden relinquishes another smile, but this time the smile is forced. He fakes it to keep his friend happy. And even though Kenneth sits just inches away, Aiden's world begins to slow down. The sounds in his midst begin to drown out until there is only one very distinct sound. Aiden places his vision upon the ticking clock once again. While the world continues spinning on around him, there's nothing there but him and that clock. Its hands slowly move from one line to the next. Each click is a thunderous hammer against a solid wall. Aiden looks around the diner, noticing each person is quietly engulfed in the shadows his mind creates. He then turns to Kenneth, who falls to the darkness as well. His face falls into ashes and rubble.

Aiden's face becomes motionless. It is frozen in time as the clocks strikes for this final time. To him, time and motion do not exist in this moment. He looks for the clock once more and notices the hands no longer spin. They stay glued to their position. It takes him a second, but Aiden is finally able to shut his eyes, breaking the zombie-like state. His eyelids clench together tightly while he places his right hand over his face, shaking himself back into existence. And as he reluctantly let's go, a thought pops into his mind. A thought that tells him that in that moment, in that room full of strangers, he has never felt more alone.

Act II
Chapter 7
You're Not the Only One on My Mind

The harsh sun has fallen beneath the earth as the night life starts to show entity. Though the day seemed hideous to Aiden, the stars burn bright with a glorious hope. Even though his sadness has yet to fully wash away, the afterhours have always treated him better. As promised, Kenneth has brought them back to their favorite bar in prayer that Aiden can somehow shake his funk off. Whether that be in some heavily poured alcohol, a beautiful woman or a combination of both, Kenneth just wants his best friend back.

Aiden ignores everyone around him. He stares into a half-empty glass and counts the seconds in his head before he pleads to be allowed to go home. He thinks to himself, he'll leave right around the time the ice cubes in his glass go from sweaty rocks to nothing more than his own personal pond in a cup. Just a few inches to his left, Kenneth is doing some counting of his own. But, instead of how many drops fall from his ice cubes, he has decided to count how many women Aiden actually has a shot at leaving with tonight. He looks left, then he looks right. Without any hesitation at all, he knows his counting is pointless. To him, there isn't a woman on earth that wouldn't be more than grateful to end up with a man like his best friend.

"Let me ask you something," Kenneth requests.

"If you must," Aiden replies.

"In the past couple of weeks, how many women have you taken home?"

"Seriously?"

"Yeah… Seriously."

Aiden roughly clears his throat. "One."

"One? As in, you've been with one per night or…"

"No. One, as in one woman within the last fourteen days."

"You mean to tell me the only chick you have banged lately is the redhead that was hiding out in your room?"

"Yeah."

Kenneth looks at Aiden in true disbelief. And as he releases a small chuckle, Kenneth looks over at the bartender and gestures for another drink for his friend.

"I think I'm good with this one drink," Aiden claims while still looking into his glass.

"One drink? Oh no…" Kenneth pauses and turns his attention to the bartender. "Get this man a shot." He takes a second glimpse at Aiden. "Make it a double."

"I'm not drinking that," says Aiden.

"The hell you ain't. Don't make me get ghetto up in here!" Kenneth exclaims, slightly changing his accent to resemble someone who would speak in such a manner.

Unable to compose himself, Aiden finally breaks his stare-down with the drink below and cracks a smile just before looking Kenneth's way.

"There he is. There is the Aiden I know and love," Kenneth says, smiling.

Kenneth takes another gander around the room before speaking to Aiden once more.

"I think that tonight is the night."

"The night for what?" Aiden asks.

"The night you get back on your horse and start talking to some lovely ladies."

Aiden gives no verbal response. Instead, he simply tilts his dome and shrugs.

"Oh, come on. I'll even let you pick the girl you get to end up with."

"I'd sure hope so, since I'm the one who's supposedly taking her home."

Kenneth grins once again while placing his hand on top of his friend's shoulder. The two quickly share a look before Kenneth wraps his hands around the top of Aiden's skull and brings him in for a gentle head-butt. Aiden, closing his eyes, allows the gesture to happen before uttering the words, "You already have one picked out, don't you?"

Kenneth releases his hold, leaving Aiden leaning and shoots up to a straight up position.

"Yup. Check out the girl at your three o'clock."

Aiden subtly turns in the direction he is given, still leaning over. Kenneth giggles whilst slapping Aiden on the shoulder, indicating he should sit like a normal human being. Now facing right, Aiden gulps just before making a face of disapproval.

"Um, Ken... I think you've had far too many drinks."

Confused by the statement, Kenneth turns and asks, "Why? What's the matter with her?"

"Cause that's not a girl."

Kenneth immediately bursts into laughter, noticing the man in reference.

"Not him, dummy. The woman behind him."

"Oh... well, that makes more sense."

"Although, he is kind of cute too."

Aiden shakes his head humorously and replies, "And if I don't really want to go over there?"

"Listen..." Kenneth says, grabbing Aiden's attention. "You

do this for me, and I'll owe you one."

"Owe me one? Why would you owe me one?"

"Because for a moment, for just one night, I can say I had the old you back. I honestly don't know when you'll be able to shake off whatever it is you're going through. And I honestly hate to see you like this, but if you can fake it for me just this one time, for my happiness, then I will owe you."

Aiden notices the sincerity in Kenneth's voice. He can tell that his best friend is truly concerned about not only his wellbeing, but his overall happiness. What is being asked of him is quite simple but would mean the world to Kenneth. Not because he wants Aiden to let go of all his pain at this very second, but because he wants him to have the willingness to at least try. He knows it is not a request made for selfish reasons but because Kenneth honestly loves his best friend.

"Fine. I'll do it," says Aiden.

"Thank you, Jesus," Kenneth says with a gigantic smile. "Let's get to it."

"Wait. Are you coming with me?"

"Yup. I want to make sure you hold up your end of the bargain."

Aiden once again shakes his head. He quickly thinks to himself that he has been making that head movement quite a lot when it comes to his best friend. Kenneth then jumps off his stool and lets out a slight, childlike wail in amusement. He then proceeds to give Aiden's butt a playful slap and speaks.

"Let's go get her, tiger."

"Oh boy," Aiden replies just as he steps off from his stool.

The two gentlemen now meet side by side and slowly make their way over to the beautiful young woman. Aiden begins to study her, from what she is wearing, to the drink in her hand, all the way to whether or not it seems she's brought friends along. She's draped in a glorious red velvet dress, of which the skirt rests a few inches above her knees. This indicates to him she is definitely trying to send signals, just not the wrong ones.

The drink in her hand is a tan yellow, garnished with an orange and a small straw to sip from. From those observations, Aiden can deduce that her drink of choice is a screwdriver and from the way she is taking small sips, she's not looking to get drunk. Just simply buzzed enough so that she can still be aware of her actions. As for having any friends along, just by her posture alone and where she is sitting, he knows she is there in hopes of meeting Mr Right. Or in Kenneth's words, is on the prowl.

As the two friends start to reach their desired location, Kenneth quickly takes a glimpse at the woman's cleavage and smiles.

"Dude, she has freckles on her breasts. You love freckles on breasts," Kenneth whispers.

"Shut up," Aiden answers, gritting his teeth.

Aiden clears his throat, now standing in front of the woman. The very first thing he notices is her sandy blonde hair. He was not able to see it before because of the lighting, but now that he can, his only thought is of how luxurious she looks. From her perfectly freckled skin to her overpowering emerald-colored eyes. This woman is absolutely stunning. Even though this woman is hands down a vision of perfection, Aiden knows immediately that she is not the one for him. But a promise is a promise, he tells himself.

"Hello," Aiden greets the woman.

"Hola, Señorita," Kenneth follows, just before being elbowed by Aiden.

"Well, hello there, sirs," she responds with a pearly white

grin.

"And what might your name be?" Kenneth asks.

"I'm Layla."

"Well Layla, I'd like to introduce you to my very handsome and very heterosexual friend here, Aiden."

Aiden, unable to compose himself, drops his head and snickers while uttering the non-existent word, "Jeez-us."

"I apologize for him," Aiden says, extending his hand, now looking at Layla. "I'm Aiden. It is very nice to meet you, Layla."

"It's also very nice to meet you," Layla says, giggling, accepting Aiden's hand.

"This here is my not-so-favorite friend at the moment, Kenneth," he adds, pointing to Kenneth. "But fortunately for us, he's gonna go ahead and walk back over to the bar and order you another drink."

"Oh?" Kenneth gasps. "Okay. I see. That's definitely a nice way to treat your best friend." He then nods just before turning towards Layla. "Layla… it was a pleasure. But if you would excuse me, I have to go erase a certain someone's contact information from my phone."

Layla just laughs some more before acknowledging Kenneth's remarks. Kenneth, in turn, looks at his best friend with eyes wide open and a ferocious head tilt.

"Hmm…" is all Kenneth utters before finally walking away. He then smiles to himself, knowing what Aiden just said was all in good fun. His happiness towards his best friend begins to build again, knowing Aiden is actually trying just because of him. He is going along with it because Kenneth means that much to him.

With a grin from ear to ear, Kenneth fluidly makes his way back over to the bar but not before he 'accidentally' bumps into the gentleman Aiden pointed out earlier.

"Oops. I'm so sorry," Kenneth says, looking down at the man, checking him out.

"That's quite all right," the man responds.

"Oh, I bet it is," he adds under his breath, walking away.

Kenneth returns to his stool and hops onto it like a child would a swing at the park. He kindly gestures to the bartender for another drink for himself, purposely forgetting his friend's earlier demand. He now turns to the newly introduced couple and watches on. He sees them engage in what seems like an intriguing conversation. Both Layla and Aiden are laughing while neither of them releases eye contact from the other. Kenneth gleams with cheer watching his best friend but is quick to notice Aiden has no real interest in this woman. He knows his best friend well enough to know when Aiden truly wants a woman. And even though he is all smiles and is doubtlessly entertaining Layla, Kenneth knows it is in a way one friend would gratify another.

Gladly enough, Kenneth is fine with that. He was not looking to get his friend to fall in love tonight. He simply wanted a night out that could help Aiden top his depression, whether that was for a couple minutes, a few hours or even the rest of the night.

"How's that drink coming along?"

Kenneth is shaken out of his thoughts and notices Aiden has returned to his side.

"What are you doing back over here?" Kenneth asks with purpose.

"Easy there, Tyson. I'm just coming over to see where that drink is," Aiden responds with a chuckle.

"Oh. Yeah. Sorry, I forgot." Kenneth pauses. "But how's it going over there with Layla?"

"She's cool. Very sweet."

"Sweet enough to lick?"

"Dude! Seriously?"

"Oh please, we both know you've heard me say worse... Actually, we both know you've walked in on me doing worse."

"OKAY! With that being said, I am going back over to Layla. Please do me a favor and order her a screwdriver and send it over. Thanks."

"You got it, dude!" Kenneth says, adding a thumbs up.

Aiden shrugs with a smile and walks away. Kenneth then watches and briskly attempts to catch a sneak at Aiden's backside. Knowing his best friend all too well, Aiden already has both his hands covering with middle fingers extended.

"I love you!" Kenneth shouts with a laugh.

"I love you, too!" Aiden screams back, refusing to turn his head.

Now, while all this is going on, a young lady currently on a date is watching from the corner of the room. That young lady is Jennifer, the friend of Marie, whom Aiden met those short weeks back. The look on her face shows that she is unquestionably amused by the antics she is witnessing. Not knowing what else to do, she cuts off her date, who is trying to engage her in conversation, by placing her hand out with her finger extended, implying that she would like him to stop speaking. Keeping her hand in place, she snatches up her purse and digs into it with the opposite hand. After a few scuffles, she finds what she is looking for. Her cell phone, of course. Without hesitation, she shuffles her screen and harshly presses down on Marie's name. She then lifts the phone and jams it up against the side of her face.

"Hello?" Marie's voice calls out from the speaker.

"You are not going to believe who I'm looking at right now," Jennifer responds.

"I am assuming the guy you agreed to go out on a date with and will later be introducing to me."

"What? No. Forget him. This is way more important."

"Wow!"

"It's that sexy guy that tried hitting on you a couple of weeks ago."

"You know I'm standing right here," Jennifer's date chimes in.

"Hush," Jennifer responds before continuing her conversation with Marie. "What was his name again? A… A something, right?"

"Aiden," Marie recalls.

"Yes. Aiden. Good memory for someone who wasn't interested."

"Shut up."

"Anyway, you should totally get down here. Like, right now."

"I can't right now. I'm working on this case and I'm getting ready for the dinner."

"Listen… The only case you should be working on is his."

"Jen!"

"You should be swinging his baton. If you get my drift."

"JEN!"

"What?"

"I'm hanging up now. I'll see you later."

"Marie. Come on."

"Bye, Jen…"

"Uh… fine. But you'll be the one regretting it later."

A click goes off, indicating that Marie has hung up on Jennifer. Jennifer releases a pout of disapproval before removing the phone from the side of her face. She places the phone back into her purse before taking one last glance over at Aiden, who is still conversing with Layla. She smiles to herself, as she too notices there is no real chemistry between the two. She is gracious for some reason, that Marie can still be in the picture.

ACT II
Chapter 8
Waiting for Something Beautiful

Only a few hours have passed since Jennifer spotted the handsome Aiden, but she is no longer in the bar where their paths had crossed. She is now sitting side-by-side with her best friend Marie. Surrounding the pair of friends is everyone they had shared a lunch with just a short couple of weeks ago, of course, including Marie's potential future fiancé. The group is sitting at exactly the same table they had before. Only this time, a giant vanilla-frosted cake towers high in the center. The words, "Congratulations Marie!" are boldly authored across the top in red, matching the fluffy rim. Sprinkles pop from the side like glitter falling from a firework explosion. Everyone's eyes continue to fixate on the glorious pastry as Christopher slowly rises to his feet, unnoticed.

"Pardon me, guys. If I may have your attention, please?" Christopher utters just after clearing his throat.

Each guest slowly removes the immersion of their eyes from the cake and politely obliges Christopher's request.

With all eyes on him, he continues to speak. "Before I begin and say what it is I need to say, I ask that my beautiful girlfriend Marie joins me at my side."

Without hesitation, Marie's eyes lock onto Jennifer's. While Marie's eyes begin to fill with hopefulness and excitement, Jennifer's tell the story of a woman who couldn't be more against the idea of her friend settling for someone like Christopher.

"Drink, please!" Jennifer shouts out to no particular server.

Marie gently giggles as her ascension is met with gentle applause. She giddily makes her way over to her boyfriend but not before she softly grazes Jennifer, assuring her that this is what she wants. At least it's what she thinks she wants. For some odd reason, just before reaching her desired station, a sense of doubt comes over Marie. To no avail, she shakes it off, blaming it on her nervousness.

Now standing side-by-side with her significant other, Marie smiles an unrestful smile and says, "I'm here."

"I just have to say, once again, how proud I am of you and all of your accomplishments," Christopher says, causing the claps to abruptly die out.

"I have to say that I honestly never doubted you for a second, my love," he adds. "And if you remember correctly, I made you an incey-wincey little promise."

No sooner than when Christopher spews out those words, Jennifer responds with a heavy sigh. She is met with a comical expression and a head tilt from her friend and a sigh of disdain from the man speaking.

"Now then... Marie? Do you remember that promise?" he adds, just before Marie's head is popped back into focus.

"Yes. I remember that promise," she replies.

"And what was that promise?"

"You promised her it was going to be a night to remember. Can we just get on with it?" Jennifer humorously interrupts.

"What she said," Marie adds, with a point towards Jennifer.

"Right... with that said," he reaches out and grabs Marie's hands. "My beautiful Marie..."

Suddenly, Marie's entire world comes to a halt. Her face begins to boil and clam up. Her glands widen, releasing pellets of sweat. Her hands start to get moist. Her nerves are getting the best of her. But it isn't the nerves you get from excitement. It's those terrible butterflies you get right before you take an exam you know you are just not ready for. She can feel in her gut that this is not right. This is not how she saw her proposal or even her life going in general. She knows her boyfriend is a terrific guy, but now is when she realizes that this terrific guy is just not the guy for her.

"I can't!" Marie exclaims.

"Oh, thank God!" Jennifer follows.

"Wait, what?" Christopher questions.

"I'm sorry, Christopher, but I just can't marry you."

"Again… what?"

"It's not you at all…"

"Yes, it is!" Jennifer adds once more.

"It's just not the right timing or feel," Marie continues.

Christopher's face changes from a look of blankness to one of confusion.

"Wait, hold on one second. You thought I was going to propose to you?"

"Yeah. Why? Were you not?"

Jennifer's eyes lavishly open while rushing her hand over her mouth, trying to keep her splits of laughter at bay.

"Well, no. No, I was not."

"Okay. Now I am officially confused," Marie adds with a puzzled look upon her face.

"What would give you the impression that I was going to ask you to marry me?"

"Well… you did say that tonight was going to be a night to remember."

"Yeah, because I was going to surprise you with the fact that I got you a new car."

"A new car?"

"Um… well, new to you. I got it from a used car lot, but it was an amazing steal."

"Oh."

No longer able to hold her composure, Jennifer's cheeks explode, releasing the liquor that was just swirling around her gums.

"I apologize for the confusion, Marie. To be quite honest, I had no idea you even thought we were at that level yet. I mean, we haven't even been together for a whole year."

"I know, I know. I'm sorry. I just thought that maybe that's what you could've meant when you said a night to remember."

"I mean... we haven't even had..." Christopher pauses and goes into a slight whisper, placing his hand to this side of his bottom lip, "S. E. X."

"Holy shit! This just keeps getting better and better," Jennifer interjects.

"Yes, Christopher, I am well aware of that."

"You know, Marie, with this misunderstanding happening tonight, I feel that maybe you should really reconsider where we are as a couple."

"I should reconsider? Me?"

"Maybe it'll do you some good to step away for a bit and re-evaluate us."

"It'll do me some good? Is that so?"

"I think so. Yeah."

Marie quickly looks over to her highly entertained friend and begins to laugh what could be considered an evil laugh. It is harsh, abrasive and rather loud. This causes Jennifer to react with a high-pitched squeal as she attempts to contain her amusing outburst with her hands yet again.

Just as Marie turns her attention back towards Christopher, a server walks by with drinks on her tray in hand. Marie reaches out and snatches the first one that she sees and proceeds to chug the unclouded liquid.

"Hey!" the server grunts.

"Charge the table," Marie responds, pausing mid-gulp.

"Marie!" Christopher says shockingly.

"That's pure vodka," she adds, pausing once more.

Marie promptly turns the glass towards her mouth, causing the remaining liquor and ice to smash against her teeth and chin. When she is finished, she removes the glass from her face and places her head up right. Small particles of ice cubes and vodka droplets slide off her jaw and crash down on the floor below.

"You know, Chris? I appreciate the gesture of the car, but with my new job title and raise I'm sure I can afford to splurge on a brand-new car," Marie says, turning towards Jennifer. "We're going. You're driving."

"Oh, thank Jesus!" Jennifer responds, hastily shooting up from her seat, grabbing both her and Marie's purses.

"Again, thank you for everything, Chris. I will definitely think about what you said and give myself those reconsiderations." She turns to the table. "I hope you all have a good night." She then turns back to Christopher. "And you have a pleasant evening yourself."

"Marie. Please don't be like this."

Marie expeditiously wraps her arm around Jennifer's neck, as the two charge towards the exit of the restaurant. They embrace each other heavily, now engaged in a wonderful laughter. These two friends went into tonight thinking this scenario was going to play out completely differently. Though they are two different minds, neither of them can help but think that Christopher actually kept his word to them, because tonight is undoubtedly a night to remember.

Act II
Chapter 9
One Night to Speed Up Truth

The unruffled night draws closer to midnight. The gentle sounds of a clock clicking and vibrating light bulbs mush together so elegantly that it seems as though they are singing a compassionate duet. Over in the foreground, sitting quietly alone, is Aiden, glancing over his family album for what seems like the one millionth time. And though he has seen it many times over, he greets each photo with a glorious smile and a mellow touch, as if he is just now seeing it for the first time. He glances over pictures of himself, quickly ignoring them so that he can get to any that contain the beautiful vision that is his daughter, Marie.

Aiden periodically takes a sip of his bottled beer, going over page by page, observing each detail in full of his Marie, from her overly warm-hearted smile, to her petite and fragile hands, to her plump and almost chewable cheeks. No matter how many times he sees her face, Aiden cannot help but fall in love with his daughter over and over again. At this point, he can admit to himself, she is one of the only two girls Aiden has ever truly loved.

Unanticipatedly, a knock comes on Aiden's apartment door. The sudden soft bang alarms him, forcing him to give a subtle jump. Unaware if he should be expecting any guests, he looks over to his clock, harshly squinting his eyes. The tame knock comes once more. Swinging his head from the clock over to the door, Aiden glares, as if, somehow, he has been granted magical powers that will allow him to see through his thick wooden door. For a third time the knock is heard, but this one is seemingly duller than the last. Somehow, he can sense the person on the other side is close to walking away and giving up.

With that in mind, Aiden debates with himself on whether or not he should continue ignoring the knocks so that this person will indeed walk away, or if he should call out and listen for a response. A final two taps come to the door, notifying him that whoever it is, they have resorted to no longer using knuckles but instead a single finger to softly brush against the wood.

"Coming!" Aiden calls out, taking pity on the taps.

Aiden places his album to the side of the couch and takes a last gulp of beer before rising from the cushions. He carefully walks on the carpet below, as if the uninvited guest did not already know he was there. The door, which is close in distance to the couch, is approached by Aiden. He hesitantly reaches for the doorknob just before a funny thought comes to mind. "This is usually where an idiot opens the door without checking the peephole and is then murdered in a horror movie," he says to himself, smiling before actually looking out into the front balcony.

No sooner than when his eyeball reaches the peephole, Aiden shows signs of confusion at the guest before him. He winces and slowly shakes his head, unable to comprehend what is going on. He then takes another look and is just as confused as he was the first time he peeped out. Now, without hesitation, he reaches down for the knob and twists while unlocking the latch with his other hand. In a simple motion, Aiden opens the door to greet the elegant and beautiful woman before him.

"Marie?" Aiden questions bewilderingly.

Standing there, in all her glory and beauty, is Marie, fresh from her interesting dinner just a short while ago. She looks at Aiden, probably more confused than he is. She isn't confused at seeing him but more so by what she is actually doing there.

"I'm sorry. I am a bit lost," Aiden adds.

"Funny... I think that makes two of us," Marie replies.

"Two of us what? Lost? Wait... So, you're saying you just happened to end up at my doorstep?"

"No," she says, turning bright pink. "I'm here on purpose."

"Okay, well then that brings me to my next question... How do you even know where I live?"

"I'm a detective. It's kind of in my nature."

"Yup. That's not creepy at all."

"I'm sorry. This was a huge mistake."

Humiliated with herself, Marie attempts to walk away but is quickly stopped by Aiden's words.

"Wait... I'm sorry. I didn't mean to put it that way."

"No. You're absolutely right. This is creepy as hell of me."

"I mean, yeah. It is creepy and a touch of crazy. But I am not complaining about it."

Aiden giggles, attempting to lighten the mood and invites Marie in. Still unsure if this is the right move, she hesitantly glides into his apartment, walking past him as he slowly closes the door behind her.

"You can feel free to have a seat on the couch. There's not much to look at in this place to be honest," Aiden says, trying to comfort his guest.

"No worries. You should see my place. It's a disaster," Marie responds.

"Maybe one of these days I'll take you up on that offer. I can return the favor and show up uninvited."

Marie stops in her tracks just as she is about to sit and gawks over at Aiden in his awkwardness.

"Kidding. Just a joke. Please, have a seat."

"No, that's okay. I think I'll stay standing," Marie says.

"Okay. That's fine too. Can I get you something to drink? Water, juice, maybe a—"

"Liquor! Any kind."

"Right on. I like it."

Aiden slides over to his kitchen area, full of jitters and nerves. Usually, he is calmer and more collected when a woman comes over, but not this time. Not with this woman. Noticing his hands are shaking while reaching up to his liquor shelf, he attempts to brush this feeling off. From the side, he notices Marie has drifted off towards the back of his living room where his sliding glass door, that leads to a back patio, stands. He subtly glances over at her and is met with her stunning silhouette standing in the starry night. He is in awe and loses focus, causing him to slip and make a vicious thud.

"Ow!" Aiden jolts.

This grabs the attention of Marie, causing her to spin around and look back at Aiden.

"You okay?" she asks.

"Yup. I'm fine," he lies.

Aiden grabs a cup from the side and slides it over on the counter in front of him. He then opens the freezer door and grabs a half-handful of ice before dropping it into the glass. He follows up by pouring some light rum over the ice and tops it off with one of his favorite sodas. Finally, Aiden reaches into a drawer, grabs a spoon and proceeds to stir the drink with the spoon's back end.

Aiden's eyes return to the site of Marie just before he begins to make his way over to her with drink in hand. He takes his time walking over, making sure he avoids all bumps and stumbles on his way to her.

"Here you go, pretty girl," Aiden says, handing Marie her drink.

Unable to spew out any words, Marie just looks down at the cup and graciously accepts. This causes Aiden to smile, because he knows she is probably way more nervous than he is.

"It's kind of quiet in here. Don't you think?" Aiden asks.

"Yeah... a little," Marie responds.

"I'll put on some music. Do you like music? Of course you like music. Who doesn't like music? I'll tell you who doesn't like music – crazy people. That's who."

"Aiden..."

"Yeah?"

"Just put something on."

"Yup."

Aiden takes his hand and dives into his pocket, hurriedly pulling out his phone. He rushes it on and promptly plays the first song he sees that he feels is right for the mood. Meanwhile, Marie takes her first sip of her drink and instantly reacts to the strong taste of rum. Her eyes immediately tighten as her cheeks come together. She then shrugs it off just as Aiden looks back her for approval.

"Delicious," she says, pulling the drink away from her face.

Aiden smiles before gently placing his phone to the side, causing the music to now play from a speaker just off in the distance.

"And a great song. Good choice in music there," Marie adds.

"Why, thank you," Aiden replies.

Marie now takes a second sip of her drink. She then notices that Aiden is without one.

"Are you not having any?" Marie asks.

"Oh, yes. I'm sorry," he says, grabbing his unfinished beer from earlier. "Cheers!" he adds, gently tapping his bottle against the rim of Marie's glass.

Both place their drinks against their lips. Aiden slowly sips on his beer but watches as Marie begins to gulp down her rum-infused soda. He removes the bottle from his lips and smiles humorously at Marie. He watches on while her tongue grasps out for every last drop, causing the ice to dance around her nose and upper lip. Noticing her drink is officially empty, she places the cup to her side and snatches the beer from Aiden's hold. She then proceeds to chug that as well but not as easily. Aiden's grin grows wider and wider as he watches the liquid in the bottle drop further and further down.

Marie quickly finishes the beer and quivers in disgust.

"Ugh!" She pauses. "That was warm... and gross." She hands Aiden the glass before thanking him.

Aiden stares down in amazement and amusement. He then walks the glass and bottle, over to the counter and rests them down. He turns around and looks back over at Marie, whom he catches subtly moving back and forth, trying to move to the soft rhythm playing.

"I bet this isn't how it usually goes for you," Marie states.

"How what goes?" Aiden asks.

"Your typical dates."

"If by typical you mean, they don't just randomly show up because they have access to some supercomputer, then, no. This is nothing like how it usually goes."

Aiden proceeds to laugh, indicating that he is just teasing Marie.

"So how does it usually go? Do you pick these same songs to mellow out the mood and get them relaxed?" Marie asks.

Aiden responds with an innocent smile, letting Marie know she's on the right track.

"And then you feed them drinks in order to get them feeling right... and just when they start to feel good and comfortable, you take them into your room and do the business," Marie adds.

"The business?" Aiden flat out laughs.

"Yeah... You know... sex."

Struggling to admit Marie has been right about everything, Aiden simply leans his back against the counter behind him and shrugs in verification. Marie nods back, filled with nerves.

"I'm sensing a bit of nervousness from you," Aiden says.

"Yeah. Just a little bit."

"I wouldn't think someone in your line of work could get nervous."

"Don't let my badge fool you. I'm still very much a human being and still very much a woman with emotions. And at this point, someone with high alcohol levels."

Aiden chuckles out loud. He finds everything about Marie absolutely adorable, from her nervous shakes to her bold remarks. It was just as he thought on the night that they met. She is nothing like any woman he has ever come across before. He really cannot help but stare at this marvelous lady standing just a few feet away. Marie quickly takes notice and tries to ignore the hole-burning glare, but it becomes unbearable.

"What? What is it?" Marie questions.

"Nothing," he says. "I'm sorry. I just find you incredibly cute."

"Cute? Cute? I am not cute! I am not some brand-new puppy or a box of kittens. I am woman who was set on a plan."

"Oh yeah? What plan was that?"

"The plan was to come here and for once do what I want. I was going to play your little game and allow myself to fall for your lines. Then eventually give you what you want."

"And if that's not what I want?"

"Oh, please. You're a guy. Of course it's what you want."

Aiden laughs once more at Marie's statements.

"So, you're going to stand there and tell me you don't want to sleep with me? You don't want this night to end in between your sheets?"

"I'm not saying that. But I'm also not, not saying that. If that makes any sense…"

Aiden gives Marie a puzzled look because even he has no idea if he just made any sense.

"I'm telling you right now that this night is not going to end like one of those cheesy movies."

"How's that?"

"You know… We drink and end up talking about our lives. Then we find out we have this incredible connection that we never thought was possible. Till we end up falling asleep together and nothing really happens."

Marie notices the eye-catching grin manifesting on Aiden's face.

"I'm serious!" Marie exclaims. "I told you the reason I was here. I'm here for a one-night stand with that dude who tried to pick me up at some random bar."

"I do have a name, you know."

"Yes, I know. Either way, this is happening. And it's happening tonight."

"Got it."

Now Marie begins to stare at Aiden. She eyes him up and down, looking at every single detail. Details she's overlooked the entire time. Like for one, Aiden has been standing there in a tank top that hugs him in all the right places. She notices his abs bulging through the cotton, giving off an impression that each one is its own individual small mountain. She catches herself drooling on the inside of her mouth and abruptly looks away, trying to focus elsewhere. Unfortunately for her, the only thing better than Aiden's abs are his arms.

They are perfectly shaped and look smoother than a new batch of butter. She gawks at his biceps that just pop and beg for her body to be wrapped in them. She then works her sights up to his shoulders and can't help but get weak in the knees after seeing how wonderfully plump they are. Her body begins to ache for his touch as thoughts run through her mind of him lifting her from the ground, wrapping his Greek god-like arms around her waist and planting a tender kiss upon her begging lips.

Marie viciously forces herself out of her daydreams, coming back to reality. She then places her hands up to her face, blocking her vision of Aiden's stone carved-like body.

"Can you put on a real shirt or something?" Marie pleads.

"No," Aiden laughs. "The object is to take off clothes. Not put more on."

Marie's fingers wander up to her scalp and intertwine with her hair. It takes everything in her not to pull out strands dangling just in front of her face.

"Fine... Fine. So, what happens now? Where do we go from here?" Marie questions.

"What do you mean, where do we go from here? Like, do we do it on the couch or do we head to the bedroom kind of where do we go?" Aiden questions back.

"No. I mean like, what's the next move? What do I do? What do you do?"

"Have you even done this before? Not randomly show up at a stranger's house of course, but actually done a random hook up?"

"No! Was that not obvious?"

"Oh... it certainly is."

"Okay, how about this? How about you tell me what it is you usually do to get these women in the sack with you?"

"In the sack? When the hell, were you born? The 1960s?"

"Just tell me."

"No. I can't do that. You'll know it's coming."

"Aiden!"

"I play this really sappy song and mention how I have only danced this song with the most beautiful girl in the world. After a few seconds of the song playing, they get into it. I tell them how they are the most beautiful girl in the world. One thing leads to another, and we find ourselves in the bedroom... Or on the couch," Aiden answers reluctantly.

"Dude, that is so corny and so cliché."

"You're damn right it is, but guess what? It works ten out of ten times."

"I promise you, that crap would not work on me."

Aiden giggles at the sound of Marie's challenge. Without hesitation, he finally stands from his leaning stature and walks back over to where his phone is placed. He rapidly presses down twice on the home button and awaits a simple chime before uttering the words, "Play my song."

The song that is currently playing promptly comes to an end and is replaced with a lighter and more sorrowful tone. Marie ungracefully breaks eye contact with Aiden and aimlessly looks around the room, almost as if she is trying to look for the sound waves in the draught around her. Aiden immediately takes notice and slowly makes his way in her direction. She is well aware of his motions but continues to play the fool. After a moment's time, Marie catches herself being sucked into the song's rhythm and charming sound. She gets lost in its gentle touch and elegantly sung lyrics. Before she knows it, the song's soft touch isn't the only one that she is feeling.

Aiden has fully found himself over by Marie's side. He eases his muscular arms around Marie's heavenly hips. He draws her in closer, almost making their bodies come together. A simple distance of a roll of quarters is the only space between them now. Unaware of where to put her hands, Marie grips onto Aiden's firm forearms and seductively glides her fingers up his bulky, yet gentle, arms. Finally, she wraps herself around his neck as he interlocks his knuckles around her dazzling waist.

Neither one is able to fight the urge to stare into the other's eyes any longer. The pair meet and grip on to each other tight. Aiden looks deep into her soul and sees nothing but pureness and perfection. He sees a goddess amongst women and can't help but believe himself as he will truthfully say for the first time, "You are the most beautiful woman I have ever seen."

Instantly, Marie's heart melts. She can sense that this was not Aiden's typical "get you into bed" line. She can tell from how choked up he is that he actually means it. And in that moment, as she stares into his alluring eyes, she honestly feels like the most beautiful woman in the world. It has been quite some time since she's felt like she honestly existed to any man, but tonight that all comes to an end. Both of them feel that extravagant bond that you only hear about in the stories told by poets. They both claim to know this night was only for one reason, but they now know that it was a lie they told themselves.

"Damn!" Marie exclaims with tears in her eyes.

"What?" Aiden asks in a whisper.

"It worked."

"It's because I meant it."

Marie instantly believes the words spewing from Aiden's lips. And while the words slip through, she starts to focus on his lips. His delicate and breathtaking lips that rest upon his face, begging for her to come in closer. The urge to deny him is truly powerful, but the temptation is a power far greater than gravity itself. The air around them ceases to exist as their bodies float through the groundless atmosphere. Everything they are feeling at this moment may seem unreal, but the one thing that reigns true is the binding of their souls in this singular nexus.

Unable to fight the yearning of their lips meeting any longer, both Marie and Aiden take a leap of faith and share what only could be described as an out of body, heart-possessing, matchless encounter. They instantly feel linked in an unearthly plane that only exists to them. The room fills with hope and love. Feelings neither of them can ever remember feeling before. Overtaken with this newly found passion, Aiden's hands slowly grace the sides of Marie's hips until they meet the back of Marie's luxurious thighs. In one simple swoop, he cups his hand and grips on to her legs, forcing them to swing around his waist.

Marie immediately obliges and locks her ankles together, telling Aiden with her legs that she isn't going anywhere. Their lips passionately intertwine and move together as if they had always belonged to one another. Marie's hands gently tickle the back of Aiden's neck and enticingly swim through his scalp, locking on to every follicle they can find.

After what seems like an hour of kissing, Marie reluctantly pulls away and asks, in her mind, the most important question of the night.

"So… Do you want to lay me down on the couch or shall we take this to your bedroom?"

"Bedroom. Definitely prefer the bedroom," Aiden responds, still in a daze.

"Okay. Go back to kissing me now."

Aiden smiles a spirit-changing smile. A smile that can only belong to a man in love. He then gracefully lifts Marie further up and begins his prance towards the bedroom door. Not once does he look up. Not because he already knows each step and where each piece of furniture rests, but because he does not want to forget one simple moment of this time. He doesn't want to relinquish a chance to remember each tender embrace of tongue and lip.

Reaching the door, Aiden kicks underneath Marie's buttocks, forcing the door to fly open. Refusing to place Marie down just yet, he walks the both of them in. Also refusing to be put down, Marie removes one of her hands from Aiden and shoves the just opened door back to its closed position. The two, in Aiden's control, make their way over to the bed. There, Aiden finally lays Marie down on his moonlit bunk while the stars gaze inside.

Their lips now pull away from each other once more, allowing Aiden to stand up straight to remove his pointless shirt. The beams of light creep in, revealing his perfectly chiseled body, causing Marie's knees to tremble and have Aiden fall back on top of her. Together they inch further up the bed, closer to the headboard. Marie reaches out and grabs Aiden by the necklace dangling from his neck and drives his lips back into hers. The two engage in their passion once more as Aiden then grabs both of Marie's hands, causing all of their fingers to interlock.

Out of nowhere, Marie pulls away. Aiden assumes it's to ask something that every woman asks at this moment. The question of whether he has some sort of protection, but he is wrong. She has something else on her mind.

"This mattress is amazing," she whispers.

Unable to comprehend where this comment came from, he just shakes his head and replies, "Thank you?"

"No problem."

Aiden tries to ignore what just took place and goes back to kissing her but is interrupted again.

"Is this one of those Tempur-Pedic ones that are supposed to go perfectly with your curves?"

"Yeah. This is one of those," he responds, slightly annoyed yet slightly humored.

"I've always wanted one of these. Or maybe even that one that is half hard and half soft. You know, that his and hers type thing."

Aiden laughs, as he is unsure of what else to do or even say.

"I'm sorry... I'm sorry. I am just ruining this moment. Please, keep going."

Once again, Aiden leans in to continue kissing Marie but is only able to manage a few gentle pecks before being stopped once more.

"Please tell me you never had a waterbed."

Aiden pulls away and looks at Marie, but for some reason, it is impossible for him to feel frustration. Instead, he giggles and says, "Me? No... okay, maybe once."

"Are you serious?" Marie laughs.

"No, of course not."

"Oh my God. Yes, you are."

"Yeah. I had one."

They both share a tremendous laugh and start on a bond of a more whimsical level.

"Do you still have it?" Marie continues.

"Nope. It exploded after five uses."

"What?"

"Just five."

The outpouring of chuckles and tears causes the yearning of physical affection to quickly vanish from the room. The two go rapidly from star-crossed lovers to lifelong best friends with common senses of humor.

"How much did this waterbed cost you?"

"Like, three…"

"Hundred?"

"No… thousand."

"Oh my God!"

"It was the most expensive week of sleep I have ever had."

The newly found couple continue to burst out in laughter. Aiden, unable to hold his torso up any longer, dives to the side of Marie, causing him to be evenly sided with her. She swiftly glances over at him before taking notice of some boxes in the corner, hiding in the shadows.

"And what in the world are those?"

Aiden immediately knows what Marie is speaking of.

"Those are my pops."

"Your what?"

"My pops. They're special little figurines that this company makes of comic heroes and movie characters."

"What's their purpose?"

"Nothing."

"They have no purpose?"

"None!"

"So why do you get them?"

"Because I'm a nerd and I love them."

Marie looks back over at Aiden and giggles, thinking he must be the cutest person she has ever met.

"You must have over one hundred by now," Marie adds, looking back over in the corner.

"I clearly have a real problem."

"What else do you collect?"

"Superhero T-shirts."

"What kind of superhero T-shirts?"

"Every kind. If you can name a hero, I have a shirt with his or her face on it at least once."

"How many shirts do you have then?"

"Probably enough to wear one each day for the rest of my life and never have to worry about a repeat."

"Where do you get these?"

"Online mostly... Clearly, I am wildly unhappy, and I try to fill my life with trinkets."

Marie begins to laugh louder and louder. Not because she thinks Aiden is immature or what some might consider a loser, but because he is simply adorable and perfectly imperfect. Aiden now joins in and titters as well. Thinking she might feel left out, Aiden decides to turn the questions in Marie's direction.

"What about you? Do you collect anything nerdy?" he asks.

"Nope. Nothing."

"Ah, so you were a middle school geek."

"No..." She pauses. "Yes."

"I knew it."

"I actually won the science fair one year. It made my mom

cry."

"What? That's pretty cool. What project did you do?"

"Research on how balance is connected to your vision. Like for instance, if you stand up on one leg and close your eyes, chances are you're going to fall rather than if your eyes are open."

"That's incredible. What other hidden gems can I know about you?"

"I do a mean impression of Penny Wise."

"The clown?"

"Yeah."

"You gotta do it for me."

Just then the world goes silent. Aiden turns over and stares at Marie as she follows. The two lock eyes again and nothing seems like it can go wrong with the night. He watches her mouth move but only hears subtle, faint sounds of her impression. Not one word sticks with him, as his jaw drops from pure astonishment at her beauty and merry mindset. The stars and the moonlight almost seem pointless without Marie being the center of their attention.

Aiden laughs, pretending to be listening, but all he can hear is the sound of his heart beating for this woman. Eventually Marie's lips stop moving, awaiting his response.

"That was the worst impression I have ever heard," Aiden chimes in.

"Oh, come on," she giggles. "It wasn't that bad."

"No. Probably not."

Again, they break out into side-splitting chuckles, unable to control the sounds that fly out from their mouths. In this moment, Marie accidentally snorts, causing the couple to gasp for breath.

"Oh my…" Aiden replies to the snort.

"I'm so sorry."

"Don't be. I think it was actually cute. My daughter does it all the time."

The laughter comes to an abrupt halt.

"Daughter?" Marie questions.

Afraid of how quickly the laughing stops, all Aiden can think is that he is going to lose Marie, just like that. He's aware not all women enjoy the thought of trying to juggle their significant other's time with their children. But what Marie says next completely catches him off guard.

"Why didn't you tell me you were a dad from the start? You would've had me in this bed so much faster."

"Wait… what?" Aiden says in shock.

"I love kids. I don't have any of my own, but I still love them."

"Really?"

"Yeah. What did you think? That you having a kid was going to scare me away?"

"Well… yeah."

"No, sir. It'll take a lot more than that." She pauses. "So, tell me about her. What's her name? How old is she? All those good details."

Aiden's fear magically washes away when he sees the excitement on Marie's face from learning he is a father. This just makes him even more happy that she wants to know about her, because speaking about his baby girl is his most favorite thing to speak about.

"Well, her name is Marie," Aiden starts off.

"I love her already."

"That's why I loved your name when you first told me what it was."

"You have fine taste in names then. But continue."

"She is four and is the most incredible person that I know. Some of the things she says and does just amaze me." He pauses. "Like, I get every parent swears their kid is the best and so smart, but even if this wasn't my kid, man... I would be impressed."

Marie's heart begins to pump faster. It is at this moment she falls for Aiden like a ton of bricks. The smile he gives off when he talks about his daughter is so radiant, you cannot help but love this man. Just the way he speaks of his Marie and lights up for her is enough for anyone to be in awe.

"Sometimes I have to go weeks, months even, without seeing that beautiful face. But when I do see her again, I fall in love just a bit more."

Marie's eyes begin to tell the story of what her heart feels. They glisten and shine with purpose and pureness. She sees Aiden for the man he really is. He is probably a man with some huge flaws just like anyone else, but right now he could not be any more perfect for her.

"It's truly amazing. She is one lucky kid to have a dad like you," Marie says. "I never really had a dad growing up. He left when I was really young. I don't even remember his face."

"I'm sorry to hear that," Aiden replies.

"Don't be. It's his loss."

"Did you ever find out why he left?"

"My mom says it's because of legal issues but I know that's just to spare my feelings. Years ago, I found out from my grandmother that he saw me as nothing more than his mistake. Turns out he had another family. A family he really wanted..." Marie takes a heavy breath. "But it's okay. If I can't have a father that can look like you do when you speak of your Marie, then I don't want him."

Aiden can immediately sense that Marie is trying to hide her true feelings. His heart breaks for her. This is a wound that runs deeper than he can repair. At least not in this one night. He can see the sadness pouring from her eyes and there is nothing that he can say to make it better. It kills him to know that some men can be so cruel and so disgusting. That they can walk away from someone they created and not give a care in the world.

"But enough about me and my daddy issues. What about your parents? What are they like?" Marie asks.

Just like that, Aiden's eyes go blank. The question he has avoided his entire life has just arrived and is asked by an angel sent to him from heaven. Unable to gather any words, he stares off into the dark abyss. His soul begins to shake inside of his body while jolts of static tickle the insides of his skin, causing bumps to cover his entire being. He tries to shake it off, but it is too late; Marie notices.

"Did I strike a nerve or something? It's okay. You don't have to answer."

Aiden slowly gains control over his body, and as color returns to his eyes, his lungs plunge forward and fill with the air he needs. He slightly adjusts his head and comes close enough to focus on Marie's loving face. He thinks to himself, if there was ever a person to finally open to, it is her. Something inside of him speaks to him and tells him that she is just as broken as he is. She is the cure for his sickness, and she can be the one to replace those lost fragments he desperately needs back.

"No… it's okay. I want to answer," Aiden finally speaks. "Where do I start?"

"Save the one that hurts the most for last."

"Okay…" He stops just long enough to gather his thoughts. "Let's start with my father."

"Okay. Lay it on me."

"My father and I have never had a close relationship. He spent most of my life at a bar. And if he wasn't at a bar, he was home drinking whatever bottle he could get his hands on. There's not much to say about him, except whenever an important event came up, like my first kiss or date or even my graduation, he was nowhere to be found. Either mentally or physically. I always thought a dad was the guy who was supposed to talk to you about your first time or get you your first puppy or buy you your first car. But not my dad. No, I had to do that all on my own. And till this day, I don't know how he was able to put so many years on the force as a cop, with all the drinking that he did."

"Wow. It sounds like neither of us had a dad," Marie adds.

"And we are better people for it."

"What about your mom then? Tell me about her."

"Man… My mom was amazing. She was so perfect and so damn beautiful. She could be having the worst day in the world, but that woman was so strong, she would never show you. I remember one time, I had to be around eight or nine, right around the time you should know how to read. For some reason I was having trouble. Not because I was dumb or anything like that, but because I was lazy and just didn't care."

"Understandable."

"So, my teacher at the time calls my mom in and tells her that she thinks I may have a learning disability and that I should be left back to redo the school year over again. But my mom was having none of that. No son of hers was going to get left back and be called slow. So that night, my mom grabbed that old book, *Go, Dogs! Go!* and she made me read that thing cover to cover. It must've been thirty to forty times, but she made sure her son could read by sun up."

"Wow!"

"Yeah. She had enough willpower for the both of us. And that year I moved up with the rest of my class, and no teacher ever doubted us again."

"She sounds like an incredible woman. But I have to ask. Because you keep speaking about her in the past tense, does that mean she passed away?"

There it was. The truth that Aiden has been avoiding for the last ten years. He knows that this is probably going to either destroy him or start him on a road of peace. But whatever the case, it is too late to turn back now.

"Yeah. She died a little over ten years back now. Her anniversary actually just passed a couple weeks ago."

"I'm so sorry. I know that must've been horrible."

Marie reaches out and places her hand on the top of Aiden's back and starts to gently caress his skin.

"You don't have to tell me how if you don't want to."

"Thank you... But I want to tell you. I feel I need to."

"Okay..."

"Before I begin, I should share one thing about my parents."

"Sure."

"See, my parents divorced early on into my childhood, so I never truly got that experience of a real family. But every so often my parents would get together and talk and pretend everything was okay. They had a unique relationship. While other divorced couples would fight and hate each other, my parents grew closer when they no longer shared the same last name. With that, they would occasionally share a night together. Only problem is my father forgot to mention that he had a girlfriend."

"A drunk and a cheater. Nice combo."

"So, ten years back I got in trouble. Over something so stupid. And even though my mom was my biggest fan and would never allow me to fail, she also would call me out whenever I made my mistakes. She punished me. In my head, I'm seventeen, just recently graduated high school. Who is she to tell me no, right? So that night I go to her, and I beg her to let me off my punishment, and she refuses. She tells me I have to own up to my mistakes and that I still live under her roof. I should've listened. I should've just gone back into my room. Instead, I yell at her. And I curse, I rant, and I rave until I can see the pain in her eyes, but I didn't care at the time. So, I left anyway. I must have been gone for three, four hours tops. And when I get back..."

Aiden abruptly stops speaking and drops his head. Marie quickly notices tears falling to the surface below while he tries to regain control of his voice. She then jumps to his side and embraces him in the most comforting hug. Just as she is about to let him know he may stop, Aiden continues.

"When I get back, there are cop cars and police barriers everywhere. I can see it all. I can see the red and blue lights flashing and the mobs of people. But I can't hear a thing. I look up at my apartment window and see cops in the frame. I ran through those people, shoving anyone that got in my way. I flew over that barrier and rammed my way in between cops... I remember getting to the bottom stairs, and I can see one officer's lips mouthing the words that I couldn't go in. I tell him who my father is, and he just lets me go past. I don't remember anything from that moment to when I saw her... just lying there... Murdered. I dropped to my knees and just stared at her beautiful face until I couldn't any more... And the one thing I kept asking was, where was my father? Why wasn't he here? How could he not be here?"

"Oh my God, Aiden. I'm so damn sorry!"

Aiden completely loses it as Marie lifts him up and places

him in her arms. She cradles him back and forth like a mother would her crying infant. She is simply at a loss for words and just cannot seem to piece anything together. After what would seem like a decade, Aiden sits up of his own accord and looks at Marie.

"It's all my fault... Had I just listened. If I had just stayed with her, I could have saved her. She would still be here."

"You can't think like that. Who knows, maybe you wouldn't be here either. And then I wouldn't have been able to meet this amazing man who has this amazing daughter."

Marie places her hands on Aiden's cheeks while gently wiping away the tears from his face, all while ignoring the tears falling from her own face.

"We find out months later, the person who murdered her was my father's girlfriend. She acted on jealousy and revenge. And again, I asked where he was, but when I finally saw him again, he had no answer for me. And it was right then and there that I decided both my parents died that night."

"I know that I barely know you Aiden, but you cannot hold on to that any more. It will eat you and it will destroy you. I know it hurts but you have to forgive yourself. Not for your sake but for the memory of your mother and for your baby girl."

Aiden knows Marie is right, but it remains too hard. It is ten years later, and the memories still haunt him. His tears begin to cease, and her hands continue to rub his cheeks and neck. He can feel the love in her hands. He has never shared that story with anyone but his best friend, because he was there with him. He lived it alongside him. Aiden knows that there is something about tonight. There is something about this woman that makes him feel loved and unique again. It is almost like his mother sent her just for him. This is a gift from heaven he will gladly appreciate.

The rest of their night continues on a much better note. They continue to share stories of pain and love. They laugh until their cheeks are numb and bloodshot. They build a bond that neither of them ever thought possible. They both agreed this night was nothing more than a night for physicality, but on this night, nothing but gentle kisses are exchanged. They continue until Aiden crashes from exhaustion. Marie spends most of that time staring at Aiden's perfectly sleeping face, begging the heavens above for this man to be real. She then tucks them both in before laying down a gracious kiss upon his forehead and resting her face against his bare chest. She softly drives her fingers over his abdomen as she slowly falls into a peaceful slumber.

Act II
Chapter 10
Now There's No One Home

The world is now a different place. It has returned to the memory of ten years prior. Aiden's mother, Samantha, sits in her favorite black leather love seat. Her hair is up in a neat and tight bun. Her face is bare but is still beautiful. Not an ounce of makeup can make her more gorgeous than she already is. On the bridge of her tiny nose rests a pair of glasses that shape her head perfectly. Her torso is gowned with one of her son's favorite superhero shirts as she watches television, while her legs are covered by her favorite and most comfortable sweatpants.

Surrounding Samantha are four plum-painted walls decorated with photos of the love of her life, her son Aiden. Pictures from his first steps to his first date, to even his most recent high school graduation. Just over on the far wall, where her television rests, is a shelf containing some of her son's action figures from when he was a young boy. To say the least, her living room and house in general are a shrine of her love for Aiden. And even though there is no love greater than a mother for her son, at times she must keep him in line.

"Hey, mom," a seventeen-year-old Aiden says, walking into the living room.

"Yes, Aiden. What can I do for you?" Samantha responds as she grabs the remote to mute the volume on her TV.

Suddenly, she takes a hard look at her son and notices that he is fully dressed for some reason.

"Um... where do you think you're going?" she asks, removing her glasses.

"I was hoping to go out with Kenneth somewhere."

"Absolutely not. You are punished and you know that."

"Come on, mom. Can't you make an exception just this once?"

"No, Aiden. I always make an exception when it comes to you. Not this time."

"But mom," he pauses, "I'm not even the one that..."

"The answer is no!" she exclaims, cutting Aiden off.

"Dad would let me go."

"Well, guess what? You don't live with your father. You live with me."

"You know what... maybe I should go live with him."

Aiden turns to the closest wall to him and unleashes a furious punch, causing it to dent as chips of paint start to fall to the ground. This quickly angers his mother, forcing her to rise from her chair and stare at the new hole in her wall.

"What the hell is your problem, Aiden?" Samantha asks, now moving towards her son. "You know, your temper has really gotten out of hand lately and I'm not sure how much more of it I can take."

"Whatever. I don't even care any more."

"Yeah, keep going. You'll end up nowhere."

"Just like my mother. The woman who couldn't even keep a drunk."

"You better watch yourself, Aiden."

"I'm done with this conversation. I'm out of here!"

Aiden hurriedly walks away from Samantha, grabbing his leather jacket and his keys that hang on a hallway wall just before the entrance of the apartment. Unable to gather herself from the hurtful comments made by her son, Samantha watches on with her jaw dropped. Her heart begins to ache in pain while she watches her son walk towards the exit. Finally, she gets a hold of her tongue and calls out in a broken tone, "Aiden!"

It's too late. The sound of the door slamming shut echoes throughout her seemingly hollow home. Samantha is left there to be alone in her thoughts, with the pain-seeking words rambling around her brain. She continues to stare where her son just stood, truly broken, not knowing this will be the final time she will ever see her son. All the while, Aiden tramples down the building's stairway, rapidly reaching the outside streets. Awaiting him is a young Kenneth, who can already tell his friend is in a bad mood due to the expression on his face.

"Is everything okay?" Kenneth asks.

"Yeah. Mom is just being a total spaz again."

"Dude. She's just being a mom. It's how she's supposed to be."

"Now I gotta hear it from you, too?"

Aiden stares at Kenneth, scarcely giving off some of his anger to his pal.

"No. No. Sorry. I won't bring it up again."

"Thank you," Aiden says, calming down. "So, where are we off to now?"

In the far distance, a dark car approaches the boys, its lights beaming down on the asphalt with purpose. It begins to slow down while the driver takes notice of the two walking along the sidewalk. Neither Aiden nor Kenneth pays any attention to the mysterious vehicle as it quietly passes. While the two proceed side-by-side, walking away from Aiden's home through the brisk wind, that very car comes to a sudden halt on the opposite side of his building entrance, parking just under a light post, of which the light gleams down upon the hood.

Suddenly, in an instant, the night is over, and Aiden is making his way back home. He walks down the street and takes notice of the several police cars parked outside. The red and blue lights circulate around the buildings, gently grazing the faces surrounding his home. He can hear the dispatcher reporting something through the open windows of the cars. He isn't able to make out much. Only what sounds like the mention of his apartment number. Aiden's eyes fly open as they take notice of a broken window up alongside the building; his living room's broken window.

Just inside, he notices a police officer investigating the shattered glass. Vicious thoughts begin to gather inside of Aiden's mind. He now directs his vision back to street level as he hastily reaches the crowd of people gathered around police barriers. Aiden forces his way through the strangers, making it his purpose to reach the front of that line.

"What's going on here?" Aiden shouts at one of the officers but is only ignored.

"Some lady… she was murdered in there," a voice calls out from the crowd.

Aiden's heart immediately drops, now piecing everything together. In one final swoop, he lunges over the barrier, pushing his way through two officers.

"Hey! Stop! You can't go in there!" one of the officers calls out, but Aiden just ignores him.

Aiden dashes over to the entrance, bulldozing his way through anyone or anything that gets in his way. Suddenly, a couple more officers snatch up his arms, abruptly stopping Aiden in his tracks.

"Let me go! Now!" Aiden screams at the officers detaining him, but they do not oblige.

Just then, a familiar face comes into Aiden's vision as he screams out, "Officer Daniels!"

A large and stocky gentleman, dressed in full uniform, turns to the voice.

"Aiden? Oh, thank God!" The officer then turns to the men holding Aiden and gestures for them to let go.

Aiden is freed and rushes over to the side of Officer Daniels.

"Jesus, Aiden, I'm so happy you're all right," he adds, embracing Aiden with a hug.

"Forget me. What's going on here?" Aiden demands an answer, pushing away. "Where the hell is my father? Isn't he your partner? He should be here."

"Aiden..."

"My mother! Where's my mother?"

"Aiden..." he says, trying to grip onto Aiden's arm.

"Get the hell off me! Where is she?"

Aiden snatches his arm away and sprints up the stairs. He instantly reaches his front door, which is guarded, but this does not stop him. He bum-rushes his way into his home.

"Mom!" he calls out. "Mom!"

Aiden looks around but can only see policemen and coroners. He begins to panic and flees, making his way forcefully into the living room. He shouts once more, "Mom!" as loud as his cords will allow.

Finally, he sees her. Lying cold and alone on their once grey carpet, now seeping with blood. Her hand is stretched out, giving the impression she was reaching out for someone. As if she was hoping to find her son there to help her, but he wasn't. Aiden drops down to his knees, causing a ferocious thud beneath him.

Tears begin to swell as his face burns from agony. The vision before him is simply a nightmare that isn't. In one final breath, with all the pain and agony in the world behind him, Aiden releases the most broken and spine-chilling cry.

"MOM!"

Then Aiden's world goes black as a harsh hush falls around him. A polite knock is heard off in the distance. A glimmer of light passes over a stone face, belonging to Aiden, while he sits at a bedside, staring into the abyss. The light, sneaking its way into the darkness, barely reveals his body, dressed in his black suit and tie.

"Aiden?" Kenneth's voice calls out.

Aiden's face stays locked onto the blank canvas of a wall before him.

"Aiden. I just wanted to come and check up on you. See if you needed something."

Still, Aiden remains at a standstill. His body succumbs to the numbness and the reality of pain.

"That girl called by the way. I believe her name was Skylar. She wanted to see how you were doing. I told her you'd give her a call later on. I hope that was okay." Kenneth pauses. "You should eat something, man. I can cook you up something. Whatever you want." He pauses once more. "Come on, Aiden… please, talk to me. Please…"

Seeing no other option, Kenneth slowly begins to walk away, briskly closing the door behind him.

"Why? Why would she just allow someone into our house?" Aiden utters softly.

"What?" Kenneth responds, reversing his actions.

"Why would my mother just allow someone into our home? Did she even bother to check who it was?"

"I don't know, Aiden. Maybe she did."

"I know my mother. She would never open the door to a stranger. Let alone acknowledge their knocking."

"I don't know, man."

"It had to be someone she knew. Someone she thought she could let in."

"Aiden, don't think about that right now. Let the police do their jobs. They are going to find whoever did this, and then they will pay."

Aiden jumps up to his feet and harshly balls up his fist.

"No!" he exclaims. "I should've been there. I could have saved her life."

"You cannot think like that, Aiden. You could have been killed as well."

"I don't care! I am not scared of whoever did this to her. I should have been there. There's no way anyone could have taken us both on!"

Aiden turns his back on his friend and walks into shadows, reuniting with the cold emptiness. His shoulders and neck roughly drop. His lips start to tremble, his teeth begin to chatter, and his hands now quiver in sorrow.

"We could have fought whoever came through that door… together…" Aiden breaks down and small ponds form in between his eyelids. "I screamed. I screamed at my own mother. She told me I was not allowed to go anywhere, and I basically told her she could go screw herself. I'm disgusted with myself and what I said to her."

Kenneth is no longer able to keep his composure and joins his best friend in his broken cry. He knows there are no words that can be said right now to mend Aiden's broken heart. Instead, he grabs his friend by the arm, forcing him to turn around and embraces him with the mightiest of hugs. This is what Aiden needs. It's not empty words or hollow apologies. It's to unleash his torture in the form of tears onto his best friend's shoulder. With that in mind, Kenneth places his palm on the back of Aiden's neck and guides Aiden's face into his welcoming collar.

It's there that Aiden wallows in pain and begs for forgiveness from his fallen mother.

"I'm sorry! I am so sorry!" Aiden utters through heavy cries and solid walls of saliva, hoping somewhere Samantha is listening.

The two friends stand there, holding one another for what seems like a lifetime. The small light begs to be shown, as they only seem to find the darkness of this night.

Out of nowhere, Aiden returns to reality. He's now lying flat on his back on his bed. To his right, Marie is snuggled up against him with her ear to his chest. His arm gently spoons her as he realizes that it was nothing more than his recurring nightmare. And though he has had this nightmare many times before, he is never able to get used to the sore throat and the profoundly swollen eyes.

His body then shakes with the fear of going back to sleep to relive those nights once again. He turns his head to his window and notices that dawn is approaching. The gorgeous blueish hue peeks in through his shades, unveiling Marie's beautiful sleeping face. Aiden then smiles to himself, pretending his nightmares have not gotten the best of him. With that, he leans over and lays a gracious kiss upon Marie's forehead, causing her to twitch and come to for just a moment.

"Hey handsome… you okay?" Marie asks worriedly.

"Yeah. I'm fine," he says while pausing to take a glimpse of her re-closing eyes. "I'm sorry if I woke you. You can go back to sleep."

"No, no. We have to do it. It's time to make love."

Marie is barely able to put the sentence together from how exhausted she is. Aiden gently chuckles at how cute she is and replies.

"Yeah. Whatever you say."

Marie is only able to give a subtle huff as she slips away, back into her peaceful slumber. As for Aiden, his day begins now. He lies there fully awake, embracing both his nightmares and his dreams come true in the same moment. He knows his nightmares are probably not going anywhere any time soon, but as long as he has Marie there to wake up next to, his life just might finally be going where he wants it to.

Act III
Chapter 11
In These Small Hours

The cold winter months now approach. The nights grow longer while the days become shorter. Though some days seem unworthy of getting up for, today is a day when Aiden is overjoyed to do so. Today is his court hearing, and even though the gusts of wind outside are harsh, the warm feeling of love and triumph fills his amplifying heart. In the far corner of the dingy courthouse basement ticks a clock. The oh so familiar hands slowly circulate amongst the numbers as Aiden's hands rumble in between his bouncing knees. Surrounding him, on wooden benches such as his, are strangers who also seem to be just as anxious. Each one just craving to hear their name being called.

"How long has it been?" Aiden utters.

"You mean since you asked two minutes ago?" Marie answers from his right. "Two minutes."

"I'm sorry. I know I can be annoying. I just hate this place already. I just want this to be over with."

Marie places her hand on top of Aiden's knees, bringing them to a calming stillness. She gracefully caresses his lower thigh, attempting to reassure him that his patience will soon be rewarded.

"What did your lawyer even say?" Kenneth now asks from the left.

"He said it should be one of the next cases the judge pulls up."

"Well, I'm sure you're next."

"That's what you said when the last four names were called."

"Yes, but I didn't really mean it." Kenneth smiles. "This time will be it. Five is my lucky number."

Just then a tall, dark, handsomely dressed and well-groomed man steps out from a swinging door.

"Aiden!" the man calls out.

Aiden's attention shoots towards the voice and he notices his lawyer gesturing for him to go over to this man. Aiden flings up from his chair and hastily spins around in order to face his two supporters. They then join him in the standing position, and each, grabs one of Aiden's arms.

"See. What did I tell you?" Kenneth says.

Aiden just smiles and nods in graciousness.

"Are you ready?" Marie asks in a gentle tone.

"I think so."

"You're gonna do fine, babe. I know it."

"Thank you, beautiful."

Aiden throws his hands around Marie's waist and embraces her with the most loving and humbling kiss.

"Thank you for being here with me," Aiden adds.

"I'll always be here for you, Aiden," Marie responds.

Aiden reluctantly removes his hold from her waist and turns to his best friend.

"If she gets a kiss, I think it is only right I get a kiss," Kenneth says.

Aiden just laughs before saying, "Not going to happen, buddy."

"Always worth a shot."

Kenneth and Aiden share a smile before the two collide with a warming hug. Kenneth then follows up by grabbing the sides of his friend's face and forcing a kiss upon Aiden's forehead.

"You got this, Aiden. I know it. I feel it," he says, now staring into Aiden's eyes.

"Try not to feel it too much," Aiden jokingly replies.

"Yeah, yeah. Go get 'em."

Aiden then pulls away from his friend and gradually walks away. Just as he is about to meet with the man that called his name, he takes one last look back. There he sees his first best friend joined at the arm with his new best friend, smiling on to let him know they will always be there for him. He too smiles back before finally turning away and stepping into his courtroom.

Already awaiting him inside is the mother of his daughter, Skylar, and her lawyer. Aiden angrily gawks at the man whose faces tells the story of a man that is willing to play dirty. He's already seen it firsthand at prior hearings. Aiden's lawyer takes notice and nudges him on towards their bench. He attempts to take a look at Skylar but all he catches is the side of her face, since she refuses to look anywhere but down at the table in front of her. Once again, Aiden's lawyer takes his attention away from his opposers and guides him over to his chair.

"Stay focused," the man says.

"Okay," Aiden replies.

Suddenly, a hush falls over the room as a voice is heard calling out.

"All rise. The Honorable Judge Jacob now presides."

Skylar and her lawyer rise from their chairs as Aiden and his lawyer just turn and face the front of the courtroom. A tall man, gowned in black, surfaces from the corner of the room and sits in what seems like a throne made for a giant. Even though Aiden has been here before, each time he cannot help but feel intimidated by the judge, who towers over everyone in that room. But it's not the distance between the man and floor that scares him. It's the power that man has. And not just any power, but the power of what is to come for Aiden and his baby girl.

"You may sit," the judge commands in a deep and forceful voice.

The entire room obliges in one fell swoop.

"Your Honor. The court presents case one two two one. The matter of Aiden Bishop versus Skylar Ramirez petitioning for readjustment of his visitations with their daughter, Marie Bishop."

"I see here that Mr Bishop already sees the child once a week, for two hours. And that it is a supervised visit by a Henry Ramirez. Is that correct?" the judge asks.

"Yes, Your Honor. Henry is Ms Ramirez's father," Skylar's lawyer replies.

"I see. And what was the reason given to the court for supervised visits?"

"Ms Ramirez was afraid that her daughter's father might abuse the child or place her in danger."

"Okay. Well, has Mr Bishop ever shown signs of aggression or ever had any issues with domestic violence?"

"Well, my client claims they have had altercations in the past."

"Your clients claims… well, from my gathering, I do not see police records or any reports of any kind to back her claims."

"No, Your Honor. She never got around to it."

"Well, if you were so worried, Ms Ramirez, I am sure you would have got around to it." The judge pauses. "I see here that Mr Bishop has submitted evidence stating that the real reason he's not allowed to take his daughter is because Ms Ramirez does not want their child around any woman Mr Bishop might be dating. Is this true, Ms Ramirez?"

Skylar's face immediately fills with a bloody crimson. Her cheeks start to pulsate as the veins in her skull begin to bulge out. She turns to Aiden, whose vision stays locked onto the judge while he tries everything not to smile in this moment.

"Ms Ramirez?" the judge calls out, readjusting her attention. "Is this statement true?"

"Somewhat. I also felt that maybe the woman he might have had would hurt my child."

"According to what I see here, that's not what you stated."

Skylar cowers over and slides in her chair at what seems like the beginning of her defeat.

Just then, Aiden's lawyer taps him on the wrist, quickly receiving his attention.

"When the judge asks, what should I say you want the visitations to be?"

"Every other weekend," Aiden spews out with no hesitation.

"That's going to be a little tough."

"If we shoot for the moon, we just might end up on the sun."

Aiden's lawyer responds with a head tilt and smile of amazement.

"I like that, Aiden. All right, let's go for it."

"Mr Bishop..." the judge calls to Aiden, immediately receiving awareness. "What is your proposed readjustment to your visitation?"

"Your Honor. My client requests he is to see his daughter every other weekend, having her obviously sleep over."

"No chance in hell!" Skylar jolts out.

"Ms Ramirez!" the judge exclaims. "You are to refrain from

using that language again in my courtroom and will not speak out of turn again. Do you understand me?"

Fear overcomes her face. Her bones and nerves begin to rattle inside as all she is able to muster up is a simple, "Sorry."

"Now… as for Mr Bishop's request. I can greatly appreciate the eagerness and the need to have your daughter by your side again, but to jump from your current agreement to one such as this is a pretty big leap."

"I understand, Your Honor," Aiden replies, trying not to break down inside.

"However, I also feel that this current agreement is not fair to you. Therefore, my proposal is this… You are to see your daughter every Saturday. You will see your daughter for triple the amount of time. So you will go from two hours to six hours, beginning at ten a.m. And lastly, these visits will NOT be supervised. You are to pick up the child alone, curbside in front of the child's home, starting tomorrow. Is everyone in accordance with this ruling?"

Aiden agrees right away with such a feeling of victory, while Skylar agrees with disdain and a sense of loss.

"Great. Then I will see you both back here in three months' time for another readjusting. Have a good day."

The judge slams down his gavel, notifying that it is now okay to stand and exit the courtroom. Aiden stands and grabs hold of his lawyer's hand, instantly thanking him for his help. His lawyer returns the favor and gently pats Aiden on the shoulder.

"Let's allow them to exit first. But congratulations, Aiden. This is just the first step… but it is a huge step."

"I know. I'm so happy and… you know, I don't even have the words to explain what this means to me. Thank you so much."

"No need to thank me. Just want to make sure your little girl has her dad," he adds, noticing Skylar and her lawyer have left. "Let's get out of here so you can go celebrate and get ready for your big day tomorrow."

Aiden finally releases his grip and steps in front of his lawyer, now leading the way to the exit doors. The two step out and are greeted by a bunch of faces awaiting their names to be called. The crowd notices they don't really have any effect on them being called, so they all go back to staring at the heads just in front of them.

Aiden turns to his lawyer and once again shakes his hand in appreciation while grinning a great grin.

"I'll see you in three months, Aiden. Until then, enjoy your baby girl."

"I will. Thank you, again."

Aiden then turns away and is embraced by the anxious faces of Marie and Kenneth. He then changes his expression to that of one that is depressed and upset. Marie and Kenneth's expressions begin to drown in his false sorrow, ready to engulf Aiden in their love and support. Aiden's eyes begin to shine as the smile of a gracious soul springs over his face. The two then breathe out a sigh of relief, joining Aiden in his happiness while he gallops his way over to their open arms and dives into hugs.

"You ass! I thought you got some bad news," Marie states just before swiping Aiden's arm with a playful smack.

"Nope. All good news," Aiden replies as he smothers in a human sandwich.

"That's amazing. Tell us everything. How did it go?" Kenneth asks.

The group allows Aiden to get out of their small huddle, having him stand perfectly between them.

"Well, I get her every Saturday, starting with tomorrow."

"So, no sleepovers yet?" Kenneth adds.

"No, not just yet. But I do get her for six hours and I get her all to myself."

"No supervisor?" Marie asks.

"Nope. No one to bother us or rush us any more."

"That is so amazing, baby. I am so happy for you."

Marie grabs Aiden and wraps her arms around him, smothering him with the most angelic kisses.

"Thank you, my love. I couldn't have done it without you," Aiden is able to utter out in between pecks.

"I am so happy for you, too," Kenneth says, snatching his best friend away from his girlfriend.

Aiden subtly dives into Kenneth's small arms, instantly hugging him.

"I'm still not kissing you," Aiden muffles, choking on Kenneth's sweater.

"We shall see," Kenneth replies, allowing Aiden's head to come up.

"But seriously. Thank you, Kenneth. Without you, I would not have been able to go through this alone."

"You'll never have to."

Aiden stands back up and hurriedly swings his arms around both Marie and Kenneth.

"I think, this calls for a celebration," Aiden says.

"Indeed, it does. Drinks on you... and maybe off of you," Kenneth replies.

"Not happening!" Marie chuckles.

As the three begin walking out side by side, Aiden cannot help but feel a tremendous weight being removed from his back and shoulders. A weight that will promisingly be left right there in that courthouse. For the first time in a long time, he feels a sense of peace, a sense of happiness. From all the unkind years, all the fallen tears and all the broken pieces of his heart, Aiden can finally feel his life being placed on a better path. His seemingly never-ending battle with remorse and pain is coming to its end.

Act III
Chapter 12
Whatever Tomorrow Brings

The dark skies have quickly fallen upon the earth below. The wind harshly growls through the air around, as the cold flows out of the mouths of those speaking. The city around is bright and decorated in gorgeous lights, giving off an alluring glow that can lift even the most crushed of spirits. In the distance, the couple that is Aiden and Marie walk linked at the elbows, staying close to one another not only for the warmth but also the comfort.

Aiden, dressed in a hooded sweatshirt and a leather jacket, cowers over a cup of hot coffee. Marie, who is adorably dressed in her favorite black jacket and a blue hood, has her face buried in her delicate, yet thermal, off-white scarf. She too has her hands grasped around a steaming cup, except her cup is filled with a delicious hot chocolate. The two walk in silence for a bit, but not because neither of them have anything to say, but because they do not wish for that bitter breeze to suffocate their throats. Even though staying quiet seems like the smart decision, Marie is no longer comfortable with the silence.

"I'm not sure when the last time that I said this was, but have I mentioned how much I really like you?" Marie says, slightly turning to Aiden.

Flustered by the statement, Aiden finds himself blushing while giving off a boyish smirk before asking, "Why?"

"What do you mean, why?"

"I mean... why do you really like me?"

"That is a good question actually. I don't think I've even given myself that true answer. But my brain just says I feel bad for you mostly."

Aiden turns and stares while the two are still in motion.

"You think you're so funny, don't you?"

"I'm the funniest girl I know." The two share a quick laugh before Marie continues. "I've noticed you've been a little quiet tonight. Everything okay?"

"With me?" Aiden pauses as Marie nods on. "Yeah, I'm okay. I think I'm just excited about tomorrow is all. I finally get the chance to have my little girl to myself."

"Yeah... I'm excited too."

Aiden abruptly stops, causing a chain reaction of Marie also stopping and then unlocking her arm from his so that she can look into his gentle eyes.

"Why are you excited?" he asks.

"Because she is your daughter. The way you speak about her is so beautiful and amazing that I can't help but want to meet her. And now that you are finally getting her back, there's a chance that I can. And if that time comes, I honestly just want her to like me."

Aiden just looks down at his half-empty cup, unable to muster any words. It's not because he doesn't have anything to say; it's because everything Marie just said brings him such happiness and joy. The ugly cold outside could never cover the glorious warmth he feels in his heart right now.

"I can honestly say that she would absolutely love you. And not just because you two have the same name."

Marie just smiles and wraps her arms around Aiden's neck with her cup still in hand.

"Well, if she's anything like her handsome father, I'm sure I'll absolutely love her right back."

"You're so amazing. Has anyone ever told you that?"

"Plenty, but you're the only one that matters."

Aiden is overtaken by a feeling of adulation. Every single nerve in his body begins to vibrate as he looks into Marie's astonishing eyes. He's overcome with the urge to just kiss her, and so he does. The two lock their lips in a tender and passionate meeting. The spark that ignites between them glows brighter than the bulbs around them. It is as if time stands still to view this purest of loves.

"I think we should go back to the bar. This way we can properly say bye to Kenneth," Marie says in a whisper, partially separated from Aiden's lips.

"We don't have to. We can just go straight to my place," Aiden replies.

"No." She giggles. "That's not very nice of you."

"He will understand."

"Aiden…"

"Okay, fine."

Aiden places a final peck on Marie's lips as she slips her hands away and returns to his side. The two now interlock their fingers with one another's and start to walk once more, returning to silence. Both of their faces give off a wonderful expression of delight, while they fight the gusts pushing against their domes. At this point the world could be overcome with an Arctic cast and it still would not be able to bury this moment.

The couple walks for just a moment before reaching the aforementioned bar. Aiden quickly takes hold of the door handle and swings the door open, allowing Marie to enter.

"Wow, such a gentleman," Marie says.

"For now," Aiden replies before adding a seductive wink.

When Marie finally fully enters the pub, Aiden slides in right behind her. Just a few feet away, sitting at the bar, is Kenneth, engaged in what is seemingly a flirtatious conversation with the bartender. He then stops to turn back after feeling a chilling breeze swivel down his spine.

"HEEEEY! Look at who came back," Kenneth shouts whilst raising his cocktail. "Are you two done being gay yet?"

Aiden laughs before taking a few steps closer and places his hand on Kenneth's shoulder.

"Isn't that the pot calling the kettle black?" Aiden asks.

Kenneth gives a look of wonder as he utters the word, "Touché." He then giggles and calls out to the bartender, "Another round, sir. This one's on me."

"Actually, no. That's okay," Aiden adds, then turning to Kenneth, "We were thinking of heading home."

"Oh, you party pooper." He pauses. "C'mon... What's one more drink?"

"Another time, I promise."

"All right. I understand. You have a big day tomorrow. Let me walk you guys out." Kenneth briefly stops before standing and shouting towards the rest of the bar, "My best friend here just got his daughter back!"

Marie and Aiden's eyelids expand with great force due to Kenneth's loudness. They both gawk at him with a smirk while subtly shushing him.

"Oh, sorry! Am I too loud?"

"Yes!" the couple exclaims collectively.

Just then, Kenneth's face goes from happy to one of panic. He starts swiveling his head from side to side, apparently looking for something. A look of sadness washes over his brow just as his friends ask, "Are you okay?"

"My jacket. I can't find my jacket. I swear I left it right next to me."

The two just laugh, grabbing Kenneth's attention furiously.

"What in the world is so funny?"

"Kenneth," Marie replies. "You're wearing your jacket."

"Oh... I knew that," he says as he laughs nervously.

Climbing down from what seems like a mountain of a stool, Kenneth is met by Aiden's embrace. Aiden cradles his dear friend close, guiding him towards the exit. He then turns to Marie and questions, "Do we have everything?"

"Yes, babe. We have everything," she answers.

The three collectively exit the bar and are gripped by the cold draft. In those few moments inside the bar, the wind went from a gentle brush to a vicious shove.

"How did it get so cold so fast? We were just out here," Marie says.

"I have no idea," Aiden replies and then turns to Kenneth. "How are you getting home?"

"Home? Who said anything about going home?" Kenneth questions.

"Kenneth!"

"What? I said I would walk you guys out. I never said I was leaving."

Aiden just glares at his best friend, saying everything he needs to say in just that look.

"Fine! I'll catch a cab. But I'm at least going to wait inside with the hot bartender."

"Okay. That's fine."

Aiden comfortably leans in to hug his friend before wishing him a good night. Marie then makes her way over and also embraces Kenneth.

"So, be honest..." Kenneth adds. "Are you two cutting out early so you can go home and get freaky?"

"GOODNIGHT, KENNETH!" the couple declare together.

"Just asking, sheesh... get home safe."

"You too."

Now walking away, Aiden lovingly pulls Marie in, wrapping his arms around her, gently rubbing her arms in hopes of keeping her warm.

"Are you okay to drive?" Marie asks, refusing to move her head from Aiden's warmth.

"I was hoping you were going to drive," Aiden responds.

"Oh, come on. I'm tired."

Aiden smiles and agrees without a fight.

"Thank you," Marie adds.

Aiden relinquishes his grip and extends his hand. Marie releases an ear-to-ear grin, quickly reaches into her pocket and places her car keys into his hand. They then reach Marie's newly purchased black CRV and separate, going towards their respective sides. They seemingly enter the vehicle at the same time, as a loud boom echoes, due to both doors being slammed shut at the same time.

"Hurry up and turn on the car," Marie says.

Aiden, with key in hand, struggles to find the ignition hole. Marie watches on as the grin from moments ago returns.

"Babe..."

"Yeah?" Aiden questions.

"This car is an up-to-date car."

"Yeah... and?"

"That means, it's a push to start."

Aiden then looks over towards the dashboard and notices the button that is used to start the engine.

"Aha! I knew that," Aiden suggests just before starting the car.

"I'm sure you did," Marie replies, now turning on the heat.

Both Aiden and Marie place their hands up to the vent, seemingly begging for the warmth to squander through. As they wait, Marie begins to look over at Aiden. Thoughts of hoping this man is real and that this could be the one circle around her head. She looks at Aiden with such compassion that it almost frightens her. The fear of giving herself to this, what seems like perfect, man makes her weak down to her very toes. She can feel the love for him grow inside her heart just by watching him try to stay warm. She knows this man can break her at any time, but the risk of trying is far worse, than not trying at all.

Aiden slightly turns his sights onto Marie and catches her staring.

"Is everything okay?" he asks.

"Of course, Aiden... I was just wondering how excited you really were about tomorrow and how it feels knowing you finally get your little Marie all alone?"

Aiden's face immediately illuminates. "Excited isn't even the word. I've fought for this moment so hard and now that it's finally here... I just have no words for it."

Marie feels the love this man has for his child. It is because of this she feels that giving him her heart will be worth the future they have in store. Her grin now extends further, as she finally lets go of all doubt in that moment. Whatever small battle was happening in her brain has finally come to an end. Her thoughts and her heart have come to a ceasefire as they both agree that she is to love Aiden more than she has loved anyone in her entire life.

"I know I said it already, but you truly are one amazing man," she says.

Aiden, unable to come up with anything to say, just stares on while his cheeks begin to fill with cheerfulness. He can see the honesty that pours from Marie's glare. He can feel the love and the tenderness that spill from each truthful word that she speaks. Though neither of them has to say it, it is at that moment they know what they are to one another. They know they have spent a lifetime looking for one another and now the search is over. The passion that is passed from one to another speaks more than any "I love you" can ever say. The words are not spoken at this time, but they know this is more than just lust or love. They know this is what it is like to find your soulmate.

Finding it the hardest thing to do at the moment, Aiden finally looks away and peeks over at the dashboard.

"Looks like it's warm enough," he says in reference to the engine.

"All right then. Let's go home," Marie replies.

Aiden reaches over to the side gear and places the car in drive. He begins to slowly pull away out of the parking space.

"You know, Aiden, there's just one thing that I have to tell you…" Marie says as her anxiety shoots up inside of her.

"Tell me what?" Aiden questions.

"Um… I want to just tell you…" She pauses. "I'm not sure why this is so hard."

"You can tell me. I promise I won't hold it against you or judge you."

"It's not that… all right… I'll just say it. Aiden, I lo—"

Instantly, the world goes silent for the couple as the rest of the world hears a horrifying smash. Off in the distance, a worried

Kenneth spins around to catch a glimpse of the terrible nightmare. It is then he sees two cars spinning out of control while metal, glass, and other debris shower throughout the air.

"AIDEN!" Kenneth shouts out from the top his lungs.

Kenneth, once in a drunken state, instantly sobers up as he dashes towards the wreck. Nothing is heard throughout town except for the sound of Kenneth screaming for help, trying to overlap the echoes of car horns blazing through the night. His tiny legs work faster than they ever have before. He almost slams himself against the now caved in driver's side door. He begins to tug and yank with all of his strength but the door refuses to budge.

"Please... God... please!" Kenneth cries out.

The door finally relinquishes its hold. Kenneth swings it open with eyes full of tears. He continues to scream out his best friend's name, but it is met with nothing. Just two pairs of eyes shut while blood flows down their faces as their hands are tightly intertwined together. Kenneth attempts to move Aiden but is fearful once he sees the extent of the bodily injures his friend has sustained.

Kenneth turns and screams into the cold air, "Someone please call an ambulance!"

Worried faces begin to enter the streets. Kenneth then turns back to his best friend and takes hold of his bloodied hand.

"Please, Aiden... please answer me."

Suddenly, a soft snowfall begins to drizzle upon the ground below. The sounds of sirens beckon from the distance. A perfect night instantly becomes an ugly darkness. The cries of Kenneth speak for the earth at that moment. And even though the world around has seemed to stop, the snowfall shows that even the most tragic of times can still give off such beauty.

Act III
Chapter 13
Just As Long As You Stand By Me

For a moment, the world is silent and still. The atmosphere remains free from commotion and clatter. That is until a vicious crash is heard. The sound of metal-on-metal springs through the air, like an amber alert for the world. Suddenly, Aiden's eyes open, causing him to shoot up off his living room couch.

"Marie!" he shouts, awaiting an answer. "Marie!"

Aiden begins looking around in a panic as he brushes his hands up against his own torso. He searches and searches but finds no scratches or bruises. Finally, his attention is called upon by Marie charging out of the bedroom.

"What's wrong? What happened?" she questions.

Aiden instantly stares at her. His eyes bounce up and down, looking for any little sign of harm or damage done to her body, but there is nothing to be found.

"Are you all right?" he asks.

"Yeah. Why wouldn't I be all right?" she questions with a fearful gaze.

"Come here. Let me look at you."

Marie hurries over to her love's side. She is quickly embraced by his warm touch as he brings her in close. Aiden continues to look and feel for himself.

"Are you sure you are all right?"

"Of course, babe. I'm sure… are you all right?"

"Yeah. I'm fine. I must have passed out."

"Did you have a bad dream or something?"

"Yeah… I guess it was one of those dreams that felt too real."

"Well, I'm here. You're here. We're both okay."

Aiden's pupils begin to shine as he stares into Marie's beautiful eyes. He gazes at her with such relief. He has no idea what to do or how to hold her. Marie easily catches onto Aiden's distress and begins to run her fingertips through his hair, attempting to put him at ease. The two stare at one another, no longer needing to exchange a single word.

Marie gently slides her palms down towards Aiden's neck and gracefully pulls him forward, planting a gentle kiss upon his lips.

"For as long as it is possible, I'll be here with you," she says, slowly pulling away.

"Always and forever," Aiden adds before engaging her with a passionate kiss.

His hands flow down her back and quickly intermingle around her waist. He squeezes her in tight and hugs her as if this were his last. He thinks to himself how precious Marie is. And even though she promises to always be there, that doesn't mean she will be. He knows that he has to love her right now, for as long as he possibly can.

"Your lips are so perfect," Aiden says while regretfully pulling away.

"So why did you stop kissing them?" Marie questions.

"I just had to share that."

Marie smiles, knowing that what Aiden says, he means.

"Yours aren't so bad either. Kind of small compared to mine but…"

"Well, that's just mean."

"I'm kidding… I love them." Marie giggles as she places

another kiss onto Aiden's lips.

Marie looks into Aiden's eyes for a moment and notices a look of wonder upon his brow.

"What are you thinking about, handsome?" she asks.

"I'm just wondering if this scruffiness is bothering you," Aiden replies, rubbing his beard.

"Oh, no. It doesn't bother me at all. I actually love your scruffiness."

"I was also thinking about how amazing you smell and how perfect you feel in my arms," he pauses, "and how each kiss tastes better than the last."

Marie's cheeks, though barely noticeably, begin to fill with rose. Her smile extends just before she buries her face into Aiden's chest. There she listens to the most beautiful sound of his heart beating. To anyone else it may seem like just any other heartbeat, but for Marie it's the most beautiful because she can feel it beating for her.

"You feel perfect to me too," Marie says.

"I wish we could stay like this forever," Aiden adds.

"I would love that more than anything."

Aiden continues to hold Marie in his arms with the intention to never let go. Her embrace feels nothing less than perfect to him. He has waited his entire life for this one moment and now that it is here, he sees no reason to let it die.

Suddenly, his attention is drawn towards the window. Outside he notices a heavy snowfall. His eyes glue onto each flake dropping. Each more gorgeous than the last.

"It's snowing," Aiden says.

Marie loosens her grip from around his waist in order to look. She too sees the large flakes gently flowing through the wind and becomes quickly fascinated. Of course, they have seen snow before, but this is the first snowfall of the year. It's so pure and elegant that it makes their moment together that more beautiful.

"It's really coming down too," Marie responds.

The couple release one another and make their way over to the window to see the ground down below. There they are greeted by a white sheet that has fully engulfed the concrete just one storey under them. It is as though the world is covered in an elegant quilt made by the finest fabrics.

"Sheesh... how long has it been snowing?" Marie questions.

"By the look of it, probably for a while now." Aiden pauses. "What were we even doing that time just flew by?"

"I have no idea," Marie ponders. "Let's go play in it," she suggests with a large grin.

"What?" Aiden questions.

"Let's go outside and play in the snow."

"Are you serious?" he asks, turning his attention towards Marie.

"Of course I'm serious."

"What are you? Twelve?"

"Ha, ha. No... come on. It'll be fun."

Aiden just looks at her and smiles.

"You know you want to, old man," she adds.

"Old man, huh? I got your old man."

Marie laughs at his remark and grabs him by the wrist. She tugs him away from the window and dashes towards the front door. Aiden refuses to fight her and follows along while questioning, "What about our jackets?"

"Screw it. We only live once, right?"

Aiden just laughs as he is dragged to the entrance of his home. In one swoop, Marie turns the knob of the front door and swings it open, causing a blustering boom. She yanks Aiden to the front and kicks him out of his own apartment to then join him on the outside. She closes the door behind her and instantly grips onto Aiden's shoulders, guiding him to the stairs, like an overly aggressive shadow, that lead to street level.

"Are you trying to make me fall?" Aiden asks while Marie rushes him down the stairway.

"Just go."

Finally reaching the bottom, the couple is met with a shin-deep blanket of white. They smile together, hand-in-hand, because they are the first to touch the pure snow. They begin to walk deeper and deeper into the street, leaving their prints behind to just continue to make more. Aiden stops and pulls Marie in and takes a deep look into her eyes. The sudden glow of the streetlamps bounces from snowflake to snowflake, causing the world to shine brighter at night than it would in the early morning. Little by little, their hair begins to change from a midnight to a pure grey.

Aiden takes the time to soak in this momentous occasion and glares down on Marie. He thinks to himself how beautiful she is. He thinks maybe it's just the cool night; maybe it's just the allure of the glowing white, but there has never been a more perfect moment. Even though it'll only be a few seconds in time, it'll be a memory he'll hold for a lifetime.

"What is it, Aiden?" Marie asks.

Aiden takes his time to gather the words. "You are simply the most beautiful thing I have ever seen in my life."

Marie gazes into his eyes and immediately feels the exact same affection. Unable to gather the words, she just jumps into his arms and wraps her legs around his waist, clamping tight. Together they spin madly into the world and fuse into one heart.

"I spent my entire life looking for you… Please… never leave me…" Aiden says.

"I'm here, Aiden… always and forever."

Aiden smiles and places Marie back onto the ground. He refuses to look away in fear he might lose just the smallest of moments from this memory. Finally, he speaks. "Well, now that we have that understanding, I'm going to have to say sorry now for this next thing."

"Wait… what do you mean?" Marie questions with a look of worry.

Aiden quickly bends down, grasping a handful of snow and instantly balls it up. In one full motion he pegs Marie with the snowball on the side of the arm and spews out a dastardly laugh. Marie's eyes open wide as a surprised look consumes her face.

"Oh, now it is on!" she exclaims.

The two run in opposite directions, trying to create some distance between one another. More snow begins to fly through the air, not only from the sky above but from side to side due to Aiden and Marie battling it out, chucking snowballs, seemingly trying to bury the other. Both of them begin to laugh as mounds of frost collide and crash up against their faces. Their skin starts to highlight in pink, but for them it doesn't matter. This moment is too magical to even wonder about the repercussions of the morning time. They continue to send waves of snow through the air, no longer caring if it's even balled up or not.

"Cease fire… cease fire," Aiden calls out.

Marie stops in mid-stride as a worried look comes over her.

"Are you okay?"

Aiden begins to walk towards her now, gripping onto his right eye.

"Yeah… can you just check my…"

Aiden instantly pounces on Marie, tackling her down to the soft ground. They simultaneously burst out in laughter as their bodies meet the frothy pavement.

"You are on a roll today," Marie is able to say, mid-chuckle.

"You should just call me butter," Aiden replies. "Get it? Cause I'm on a roll."

"So smooth too."

Aiden stares into Marie's eyes while the snowfall from above gets heavier and heavier. The two keep their sights locked on to one another, even through the thick flakes are attempting to enshrine them in this moment.

"Can I ask you something?" Aiden requests with leg and arm over Marie.

"Sure."

"Is there any time you don't look beautiful?"

Marie instantly blushes and smiles. Having no clue what to even say, she grabs Aiden around the back of his neck and drags him in for a kiss. Their lips engage in a sweet and passionate affair. They can feel the snow slip in between each kiss but to no avail, they proceed on.

Suddenly, Aiden pauses and quietly looks around. Marie watches on, once again concerned something is wrong.

"Why do you keep giving that look?"

"I just noticed there is not one single car in this parking lot," he responds, turning his head from side to side.

"You're right," Marie adds, now following his movements. "And your apartment light is the only one on."

"Were we the only ones unaware of this storm or something?"

"It looks like it."

"How bad is it supposed to get out here anyway?"

"I really have no clue, babe. Maybe we should get back inside and check the news."

Aiden nods his head and springs up to his feet. He dusts himself free of most of the snow and extends his hand to Marie. She gratefully accepts and props herself up by his side.

"Oh yeah. I forgot to tell you…" Marie adds.

Aiden turns and awaits her words. Instead of hearing her peaceful voice, he is greeted with one last snowball atop his head. Marie instantly laughs and walks away.

"Okay… I deserved that," Aiden says to himself.

He then follows behind Marie as she now makes her way back up the stairway. The two hold tight onto the railings, avoiding any slippery steps. Aiden catches himself staring at Marie, but not in a way a man usually would check out a woman. He simply cannot fathom how even the way she walks sends his heart into irregular beats. Little does he know, Marie is thinking the same, by just hearing him breathe slightly heavier breaths due to the climb. Something so simple as his breathing is making her skin fill with bumps that only he can put to rest with his touch.

They now find themselves in front of the apartment door as Aiden calls out, "I left it unlocked."

The two swarm inside and are engulfed by the welcoming heated apartment. Marie enters first, making room for Aiden to follow. In almost a coinciding moment, Aiden enters the room, closes the door and grabs Marie to pull her in close. He wraps his arms around her waist and says, "I had a dream that I lost you." He then briefly pauses. "We were about to drive back here. I was pulling out of a parking spot and out of nowhere, this other car rams us from the side… I looked at you for just a moment before my eyes got too heavy. And all I could do was feel helpless because I couldn't save you."

"Was this the dream from earlier?" she asks.

"Yes."

Marie just looks on at his fearful glare and brushes the back of his scalp.

"But we are both okay and just like I said before… for as long as I have a say in it, you will never lose me."

Marie gently pulls Aiden forward, placing a tender kiss on his forehead. That kiss is instantly met with a cheerful expression. His grip around her waist grows a little tighter, giving the impression that her words are felt and that he will never let her go.

"I have a great idea," he says.

"What's the idea?"

"How's about you get out of those wet clothes, and you let me watch?"

"Oh yeah?"

"Yeah."

"Sounds like a good idea to me."

Marie then places yet another kiss upon Aiden's lips, just before slipping away through his fingertips.

"By the way, you have a message," she adds.

"What?"

"On your house phone. The message button is blinking."

"Oh… okay. I'll listen to it now. Don't get undressed yet."

"Okay," she says with a little laugh.

Aiden gracefully glides over to the phone and picks it up from the receiver. He then places the receiver up to his ear and pushes down on the message button to listen. Immediately, a sweet and lovable voice chimes through.

"Hi, daddy!" Aiden's daughter's voice plays, causing him to place his hand over his mouth. "I just wanted to call you and say

I miss you." Aiden's eyes begin to swell while tears form and instantly glide down his face. He knows Skye would never allow her daughter to call him. "And that I am so excited to see you tomorrow."

Aiden grows confused and is trying to piece everything together.

"Aiden!" Marie calls out but is ignored.

"Okay, daddy. Have a good night."

"Aiden!" Marie calls out once more.

"I love you!"

"Aiden!"

This time the call grabs his attention and he slowly lowers the phone down. He looks on at Marie, who has the most frightening look glossing over her face. Blood begins to flow down her face and torso from out of nowhere.

"What's happening to me?" she questions.

Aiden drops the phone, allowing it to clash to the floor. His eyes widen with panic, only to notice that blood is also consuming his being.

"It was real... it wasn't just some dream."

"What do you mean, it wasn't a dream?"

"Us... getting into the car. You asked me to drive, and we pulled off and then we got hit by another car. Don't you remember?"

"No... the last thing I remember is running out of the bedroom because you were screaming for me."

"What do you remember before that?"

"I... I..."

"Just breathe. Take your time."

Marie pauses while grasping at her chest, hoping to close her wounds. With tears in her eyes, her memory slowly returns.

"I made you drive my car... We had just left the bar with Kenneth. I remember that I was about to share something with you and then everything just went black."

"Yes. That's when we got hit."

They both stare at one another in fear. Both of them are equally confused and equally petrified. They notice that their once open gashes have miraculously vanished. The once pouring blood seems to have been washed away.

"Aiden... what's happening?"

"I don't know." Aiden pauses. "But I do know that this is my fault. Whatever is happening is because of me."

Marie immediately notices the pain and guilt behind Aiden's eyes. And instead of trying to comfort him with her words, she easily steps towards him and hugs him. She gently strokes his back as Aiden begins to tear up, afraid of what is to come next. Not a single word is exchanged between the two. They both just close their eyes for a moment, which begins to feel like an eternity.

Suddenly, the sounds of the world around them begin to change. The silence is quickly overcome with machines beeping and mumbled voices that sound as if they are being played over a loudspeaker. Both Aiden and Marie become aware of this and open their eyes in unison. It is then they notice they have gone from Aiden's comforting apartment to being transported to a hospital.

"I don't understand what's going on," Marie says, slightly pulling away from Aiden.

She starts to take notice of where she is now. Her mind fills with depression by just looking around at the typical blue-and-white tile setting of a hospital floor. Aiden, on the other hand, focuses on the disheartening off-white walls. They casually get a better look at their surroundings.

"I know you said the crash wasn't a dream, but could this be a dream now?" Marie questions.

"I really doubt that," Aiden responds.

Aiden gradually walks away from Marie and begins his search for something. He begins to walk the gloomy halls, poking his head into different rooms. Perplexed by what is taking place, Marie watches him before finally calling out, "What are you looking for?"

"I'm looking for us."

"Us? What do you mean, us?"

Marie now follows behind Aiden for just a moment but freezes upon finding a familiar face. "Kenneth!" she screams out. Kenneth hurriedly swings his attention towards Marie's direction, seeming to have heard the call. She immediately smiles, thinking to herself that somehow all of this is just a crazy daydream, and they are there together, but she is wrong.

Marie's expression quickly changes when Kenneth walks right past her suggested embrace. It is there she watches her friend consult with a doctor instead.

"Is everything okay? Are my friends going to be all right?" Kenneth asks.

"Well, the passenger, the female, just got out of surgery. She is stable at the moment. As for the driver, he's still in surgery. His case is a little more touch and go. The oncoming vehicle collided with his side, causing him to have sustained a few more injuries."

"What does all of that mean?"

"As of right now, all we can do is perform the surgery on him and take it from there."

Marie backpedals away from the ongoing conversation and makes her way back to Aiden. Each step she takes towards him, the more and more anxiety fills within her.

"He couldn't hear me. He couldn't see me," she says.

"He might not have, but I can," Aiden says, pointing inside one of the rooms.

Marie walks over and peeks inside. There she's met with a nightmare of a sight. Right there before her is her own self. Her body is laid across a bed with wires injected into her arms and a heavy tube extending from her mouth. She looks on in fear at her own body grasping for life as her chest slowly rises up and falls back down. Marie then enters the room to stand alongside herself. Unable to comprehend what is transpiring right in front of her, she looks back at Aiden for reassurance. He too has no understanding of what is going on. His eyes just aimlessly bounce between both versions of Marie until he is no longer able to withstand it.

Aiden scrambles away and walks off into the corridor. He keeps his head down, refusing to engage with this nightmare he is in. That is until he hears a voice say, "Have you ever seen someone survive a crash like this?"

He begins to search for where the voice came from. He peers into room after room. He looks at door number after door number and just as he is ready to collapse right there and give up, he finally stumbles upon the room where doctors are currently working on his body. He looks on, terrified at the sight before him. He witnesses his body being opened and repaired from the inside out. He begins to tear up at the thought of this operating table being the final spot he's able to lay his almost lifeless body. Only able to watch his body lose color for a moment, Aiden finally turns away and re-enters the halls.

He dashes away from the room and strides towards an empty bench further down the hallway. He promptly crashes down onto the seat below and buries his face in his palms. He silently shakes from the visions he just witnessed. As hard as he may try, he just cannot seem to get what is taking place right now. Though the time seems to be moving as normal, to him each second passes along like another lifetime.

Suddenly a hand falls upon his neck, causing him to rapidly look up. Marie has now rejoined Aiden's side.

"Hey…" he says. "How's the second you doing?"

"I'm not too sure really. I left right after you, hoping I would find the other you," she replies as she takes a seat. "But by the looks of it, you already did that."

Aiden looks on, briefly filled with hope. He leans in and gently brushes his lips up against her forehead.

"Do you think we are still alive… like, we still have a chance to make it back out? And we can live our lives together?"

"There is always a chance. But we also have to face the fact that we might not."

"I know."

"And if for some reason this is where we end up, this is where we stay… there is no one I would rather be with," she pauses for a gulp, "than you."

The couple look at one another and slide into each other's arms. Aiden swings his arm around Marie and gently coddles her. Together, they begin to tear up once more, praying that this truly is not it for them. Their eyes shut in unison, and as their world fades to black, time flashes forward.

Just then, a breeze flourishes over them, causing their eyes to unfasten. Kenneth appears before them. They see him briskly walk past, clearly making a gesture towards a particular room. Aiden briefly looks at Marie and whispers, "Stay right here. I'll be back."

Aiden springs up from the seat and races behind his friend. He shows looks of concern and bewilderedness. Kenneth, slowing down, enters one of the rooms as Aiden proceeds from behind. It is there that both of them are greeted by Aiden's broken body. He, just like Marie, is covered in wires and a tube that is assisting his breathing. He looks on at Kenneth, who is inches away from breaking down but doesn't. He witnesses his friend remaining calm and together while grabbing a chair and placing it at Aiden's side.

Kenneth now falls into the seat and grabs Aiden's lifeless hand.

"Hey, hubby..." he says. "I'm not too sure if you can even hear me but the doctors say there is a slight chance that you can. And if that's the case, then there's just a few things I want to say to you." Kenneth briefly pauses in order to regain his composure. "Do you remember that time back in high school that I was just starting to come out of the closet, but I was still a little scared? And you looked at me and told me that no matter what, you were proud of me and that I was your hero for coming out? It was in that moment that you were the one that became MY hero. You became my best friend! And from that moment on, my life became so much better because you were in it." He pauses once more. "I can't even remember if I ever thanked you for that."

Kenneth stops for a moment, attempting to shake off the tears and to clear his throat.

"So, I want to say it here and now. Thank you, Aiden."

Aiden, watching on, steps a little closer to his friend in the chair and simply nods.

"The doctors say they can't even understand how you're breathing right now. They can't understand how you are alive. But I do! You're the strongest man that I know. I've seen you fight the toughest battles in life and walk out on top. So do me this favor... and fight one more time... Walk out on top one more time... Come back... please, Aiden... You are my best friend. I need you and I love you!"

The room grows still, and a violent hush falls around them. Aiden, fighting back a harsh cry, looks down at Kenneth and speaks.

"I love you too, Kenneth. I will miss you most of all."

Aiden silently leaves his friend's side and walks back off into the corridor he was previously in. Just outside the doorway, Marie awaits him. She looks on at him with tears of doubt as she expresses her worries through sobs. Aiden gazes upon her skin and takes notice to the returning color. And as quickly as he notices her bright tinge, he realizes his is getting duller.

"I don't want to stay here, Aiden," Marie says.

"You won't. I promise."

Aiden grabs Marie by her hand and pulls her along towards another room. Aiden gracefully pushes the door open and unveils a gorgeous garden. Somehow the storm from outside has vanished and they are surrounded by blooming roses and luscious blades of freshly cut grass. Hand-in-hand the two step out, transporting from the death-filled building into a life-filled oasis.

Marie gently squints and has somehow been redressed in a long and elegant white dress. Her hair is done in bouncy, angelic curls. Her face is dazzling with the perfect amounts of eye shadow, lipstick and blush. She looks over at Aiden, now handsomely dressed in an exquisite suit. His hair and beard are cleanly cut and perfectly groomed to her liking. She is simply mesmerized by her new surroundings.

"This is all too beautiful. What is this place and how did this all happen?" she questions.

"This is where I pictured it happening. This is what I pictured us looking like," Aiden responds.

"What do you mean?"

"Our wedding."

The two easily venture off further and further into the garden, until Aiden forces them to stop just under a delicately decorated canopy, a canopy bathed in all kinds of colorful flowers and dimly lit lights. Marie just gawks on in amazement as Aiden grabs her by both of her hands and stares into her loving eyes.

"This is where I wanted to start the journey of the rest of our lives together. This is where I wanted to tell you that every day I want to look into your eyes and feel my heart break. I want to feel it break from the thought of not being able to see you again, only to wake up the next morning and see you still there."

"But I told you Aiden... I am not going anywhere."

"I know you told me, but now I need you to make me some promises." He pauses. "I need you to promise me that no matter what, you will come visit this place."

"I can promise you that WE will come visit this place."

"Promise me that you'll always have that beautiful smile and never worry about what life was supposed to be."

"Aiden. Why are you talking like that?"

"Most of all, promise me you'll get this fixed."

Aiden reaches out and grabs her nose, making a honking sound. Marie gives a brief smirk but refuses to let go of everything Aiden has just requested.

"You still aren't telling me why you're saying these things or why you are saying it the way you are saying it."

"Because, Marie... this is where you leave me."

"What the hell do you mean, this is where I leave you? I'm

not going anywhere without you," Marie says angrily.

"You can't stay here, but I will."

"Why are you saying this to me?"

"My body... my being... I can feel myself getting weaker and weaker. And then I look at you, and I can see the color returning. I can see how close you are to going back."

"None of that matters, Aiden. I am not leaving you... Wherever you are is where I am meant to be."

"Marie... you don't have a say in the matter... and even if you did, we both know this isn't where you belong."

Marie takes a few steps away from Aiden and places herself down on the grass below. She immediately begins to cry and gently rock back and forth. Shen then begins picking up blades of grass, removing them from their roots and tossing them to the side. Aiden makes his way over and joins her on the ground below.

"I want to stay here with you," she says.

"I know you do. And as much as I want to be selfish and keep you here, I can't. And you can't."

"Yes, I can! I can stay!"

"No, you can't. You don't belong here. Wherever HERE is, you can't stay."

"Why, Aiden? Why can't I stay?"

"Because this is all my fault."

"Stop saying that. No, it isn't... I can't do this. I can't leave without you. I won't be able to live without you now."

"You're not going to."

"So come with me!"

"I can't go back with you."

"Tell me why then."

Aiden cowers over Marie and enshrines her in his arms. His

muscles enclose her in his tomb of a body. He hugs her tighter than anyone has ever hugged her before. He tries to reassure her that all of this will be okay. Then he whispers into her ear.

"I don't have all of the answers. At least not yet. But I know that this is what I must do... what we must do. And I need you to believe in me... please."

"Okay..." Marie says, voice cracking and collapsing. Her young sobs now transform to growing moans and whimpers. "Just please come back to me. Please come back home so that we can come back to this place, and we can relive this nightmare as our dreams come true... Promise it to me, Aiden."

"I promise, Marie... I promise," Aiden says with an honest smile. "Now breathe and close your eyes."

Marie inhales a broken breath and gently exhales a painful sigh. Slowly but surely, she regains her composure. And just as the world is about to go still, she hears Aiden say, "I love you, Marie... for the rest of my life."

Marie swings her eyelids open to see the man that uttered those words but sees nothing more than drywall. She calmly moves her head to the side and comes to the realization that she is now awake on top of her hospital bed. She forces her eyes closed in hopes of returning to the world she just knew but is greeted by nothing more than dull plaster. She then casually takes a soft breath as a single tear falls from her eye and utters into the air above, "For the rest of my life."

Act III
Chapter 14
I'd Give Up Forever to Touch You

Now without Marie, forced to walk the halls of the gloomy hospital, Aiden wanders around the land of the living unseen. He sees different faces walk in and walk out of the waiting room and hallways. Though he finds himself completely surrounded by all these people, he can't remember a time he's felt more alone.

The only time that he feels somewhat at peace is when he stands outside Marie's bedroom door. That is where he stands now. He watches on like a personal guard, naming himself Marie's very own angel. He watches her now and smiles to himself, happy to see she is not alone. Her best friend, Jennifer, has arrived and now accompanies her, seated at her bedside. Aiden can't help but feel warm and loving, watching Marie crack what seemingly is a smile. He can tell she feels just as broken as he does but any little sign of hope that comes to her face brings him some too.

"She's very pretty," a voice calls out.

Aiden viciously swings his head around, looking for the person who just spoke those words.

"Who said that?" he calls back.

Receiving no immediate response, Aiden walks away from his post and proceeds into the crowd of people in the waiting area.

"Is anyone else here?" Aiden calls out once more.

Aiden still hears nothing in return and walks a little further. Suddenly he hears a voice call from behind.

"I guess I'm not the only one here."

Aiden turns back to come face-to-face with whom the voice belongs to. There, seated just below him in one of the waiting room chairs, is a young man with skin of bronze and hair of wool. Judging from his slight accent, Aiden assumes he is of Hispanic heritage. The man is dressed from head to toe in a blue and orange baseball uniform. One could easily assume he isn't just a fan but an actual player.

Unable to gather any words, Aiden just continues to stare on with confusion.

"Yeah. That was the same face I had when someone first spoke to me in here," the man says.

"Wait... you can see me?" Aiden questions.

"Obviously. How else would I be speaking to you right now?"

"Touché."

Aiden slightly shuffles towards the man, unsure of how to approach him.

"Please, have a seat," the man says, gesturing to the chair next to him.

Aiden obliges as he extends his hand and says, "I'm Aiden, by the way."

"Nice to meet you, Aiden. I'm Tony, Tony Garcia."

Tony then too extends his hand, greeting his new comrade with a firm handshake.

"So, you've been here a while, I'm guessing," says Aiden.

"A little over three months now."

"Do you know what this place is? Do you know how we get to go home?"

"I don't really know what to call this place or how we get out, but what I do know is we aren't alive, and we also aren't dead either."

"So, there's a chance to go either way."

"I guess so, yeah," Tony says. "What's your story anyway?"

"What do you mean?"

"I mean, how did you get here? What caused you to be walking these halls?"

"Oh... I was in a car crash. I was driving and we got hit from my side."

"I guess that kind of explains why you're still here and your girl was able to go free."

"I guess so too... Wait... you said something about other people in here too. Where did those people go?"

"Honestly... most of them passed. But there was this one little girl who went back. She's the reason I still haven't given up. She's why I believe there is still a shot."

"Well... here's to that shot."

Off in the distance, Aiden notices Kenneth enter Marie's room. He is instantly overcome with curiosity. The urge to get up overflows inside of him to the point where he can no longer withstand it.

"I know you want to go and see what he has to say, so go ahead," Tony says.

Aiden instantly shoots up from the chair and zooms toward the entrance of Marie's room. Getting there rather fast, he quietly stands right outside the threshold, refusing to fully enter. Instead, he just gazes in and listens in on the conversation taking place.

"I think we really need to talk about Aiden's condition," Kenneth says to Marie while Jennifer listens in.

"What do you mean, his condition? Did he wake up?" Marie

asks with a frightened look.

"No, my love. He's not awake. It's actually…" Kenneth gulps. "It's actually the opposite. The doctor said he's not doing so well. It's getting harder for him to breathe, even with being on the respirator."

"Do they think he's going to be okay?"

"They don't know actually. It turns out some of the injuries are worse than they thought."

"What do you mean?"

"The doctors said something about kidney failure and him needing a transplant. I honestly couldn't function while they were talking. All I know is without one soon, he's not going to have much time."

Both Marie and Jennifer's eyes begin to water as those horrific words bounce off Kenneth's lips like a wrecking ball to the walls of their hearts.

"I have to see him," Marie declares.

"I'm not sure they are going to let you do that, Marie," Kenneth responds.

"I don't care if it's something they are going to let me do. I need to see him."

Seeing her best friend consumed with unbearable pain, Jennifer interludes.

"Don't worry. We will find a way to get you to him. Won't we, Kenneth?"

No words are said by Kenneth, just a simple nod of surrender.

With Aiden still watching on, he suddenly feels a hand fall upon his shoulder in the means of comfort.

"I'm sorry, man. I'm sure that's tough to hear," Tony says, trying to pull Aiden away.

"Like you said, there's always that little bit of hope, right?" Aiden responds, obliging to Tony's subtle yank.

"How's about we head outside for some air?"

"Does that make a difference for us?"

"Not really, but it's the sentiment that counts."

Aiden nods and begins to walk side-by-side with his new buddy. The two men walk from room to room, hall to hall, ignoring the dreary darkness that surrounds them in that hospital. They pretend that nothing is wrong for just that moment, knowing very well that everything is. The two men hastily exit the building and enter a small terrace just off to the side of the building.

"It's a beautiful night, don't you think?" Tony asks.

Aiden simply nods.

"You know, I must have been out here over a hundred times now. And every time I am, I tell myself the same thing," he adds.

"And what's that?" Aiden asks, placing his hands into his pockets.

"I tell myself that if I can live, I will never take another day for granted. That I will love every single day. No matter how ugly it may seem. I swear that I'll love every drop of rain, every blazing summer day, every freezing snowfall." He pauses to point out the falling flakes. "I spent my entire life going from day to day, ignoring the smallest of things. Whether that was a bee buzzing, the wind blowing or even a leaf crunching underneath my foot. I promise I will never take those moments lightly again."

Aiden takes in everything he just heard and gently nods in agreement. Everything Tony stated also falls true onto him. Aiden knows, that if somehow he manages to rejoin his body, there is not a single moment that will pass him by that he won't cherish or love. No matter how hideous the day may seem.

"Tony… can I ask you something?"

"Yeah. Of course."

"Do you know what happens next? Like, if we die, where do we go?"

"I honestly do not have an answer for you. I guess you have to go on with your faith. You know… what you were brought up to believe. But honestly, I'm not ready to find out."

"I hear you, man. It's not time to find out just yet."

The two look out at the surrounding city. They take in the world for what it is and all the beauty that it has to offer. They stare out into the glorious lights glowing throughout the world just off in the background. They stop for a moment to think to themselves that if this is truly it, if this is all that is left for them, then they will consume all that they can and as much as they can before it's taken away right before their eyes.

"I'm going to head back in. You coming?" Aiden asks.

"You go ahead. I'll be right in."

Aiden smirks just as he walks back into the hospital. He thinks about all the beauty that he just had his sights on. It was just a few moments ago that these halls seemed so bland and colorless. Somehow, they have become full of life and light. Aiden sees now that all it takes is a quick glimpse at the world in a different light to see it for all the real beauty it contains. He smiles to himself as he begins to feel hope for the first time since being in this world before death. That is until he comes across his room, where he finds himself together with Marie. His heart immediately breaks from seeing her sit there in a wheelchair, barely holding together, while she coddles his hand in hers in what seems like the darkest of rooms.

"Hi, baby…" she says while Aiden listens on. "You know,

this might sound crazy, but looking at you now, you are still the most handsome man I have ever seen… but I'm not here to fill your already big ego with more compliments." Marie pauses in order to release a gentle sob. "I'm here because I needed to see you again. I had to see for myself that this nightmare is actually true…" The crying begins to increase. "I watch Kenneth constantly lie to me while trying to put on his best poker face, but I know deep down he's petrified at the thought of losing his best friend. Just like I'm petrified at the thought of losing my soulmate…"

Marie then violently wipes some of her tears away. "But you're not going to leave us just yet. You can't. So, I need you to open your eyes now, baby. I need you to show me those gorgeous hazel browns and smile that smile I love so much. Please, just look at me once more. Look at me with that look of fear of losing me so that I can tell you that I will never leave you, Aiden. I swear, if you just come back to me, I'll never let you go again. I'll be yours… for the rest of our lives."

No longer able to hold her composure, Marie breaks down into pieces, releasing a river into Aiden's hand as she gently rubs it against her cheek. With each tear, a vicious sob comes along while she tries to fight back the echoes bouncing from the walls. Aiden, watching from behind, slowly makes his way towards Marie, begging the beings above to allow him to console her. But his prayers go unanswered.

"You might not see it, but the beauty in this is knowing there is someone who can love you that much," Tony calls out, joining Aiden from behind.

"You may see beauty. But I see nothing but pain," Aiden replies.

"Don't think like that."

"It's hard not to."

Aiden continues to look down at Marie, still begging to return to her side. He knows deep down he's not and probably never will. So, with a deep breath he gathers all his love and emotions for one last, "I love you, Marie. For the rest of my life."

Aiden turns around and leaves his love alone to join Tony in exiting the room. The two men slowly walk away from the doorway and make their way over to a seemingly comfortable couch. Together they sit, just before Aiden turns to Tony and asks, "You know, all this time has gone by and I have yet to ask you, how did you get here?"

"Me... I was shot... twice. It was one of those moments you hear about on TV where a crazy fan becomes so obsessed, they seem to think taking a life will be meaningful. It's amazing to me how this world functions sometimes."

"Wow! I am so sorry. Do you know if you're going to make it?"

"Like I said, I try to keep hope alive. To be honest, I stay away from my room."

"Why is that?"

"I don't want to hear any bad news or have anything stop me from holding onto this faith I have."

"I don't know how you do it, man. How you can be here and still be trying to see the beauty and hope in the world. How you refuse to give up."

"If I don't do it, who will?"

A loud echo beams through the hall. The sounds of monitors and footsteps consume the corridors. Loud and ferocious beeps gleam from eardrum to eardrum. The two men hear doctors' panic. They now come to the horrible realization that one of their lives is over.

"It was really good talking with you, Tony."

"Likewise, Aiden. And remember… no matter what, never give up hope."

The men nod at each other and say their goodbyes. Aiden then turns away and closes his eyes, squeezing them tight in order to stop himself from falling apart. He knows deep down Tony is a great man and would love nothing more than for them both to live on, but a small and selfish part of him can't help but to cry out for the return of his life. Slowly the sounds from around drown out into the midst of a world as a cool darkness falls upon the ground below. Soon the only sound that is heard is that of a clock ticking. A ticking that booms with greatness. A ticking that gradually slows down to the point of non-existence. Aiden unhurriedly opens his eyes to a world of nothingness. A world abandoned. Everything he has ever known, everyone he has ever loved, is now gone. Just like that, Aiden has now faded away from hope.

Act III
Chapter 15
May Angels Lead You In

The world is nothing but darkness. Space and time are just an illusion to Aiden, who just stands there, refusing to loosen the grip his eyelids hold. Little by little, he relaxes the muscles on his face, allowing them to rest as though he were asleep. No sooner than when he comes to a full relaxing state, the sound of a booming roar blazes through the sightlessness.

Aiden swiftly opens his eyes to witness what is causing such an eruption. It is then that he sees a large locomotive easily pulling in right in front of him. The horn continuously sounds off, purposely seeking Aiden's attention. Dazed and confused, Aiden watches on while the head of this train travels past him. With the most bewildered look upon his face, he looks at the train from end to end. With what seemingly is the middle of the train, he can't help but be under the impression that the front and back carts are miles away from each other, even though they are not.

Slowly but surely, the caboose comes to a halt. Unsure of what to even do, Aiden attempts to stare into the windows of the door just before him. Abruptly, the sound of air being pushed out surrounds Aiden as the sliding doors open, releasing a gentle mist. The doors calmly open while leaking a light chime, indicating that it is now safe to board the cart. Aiden hesitantly steps forward and only looks in, battling with himself to fully enter the train. It's not until he sees a certain book, just resting there on a seat, that he completely penetrates the doorway. He inches closer and closer, attempting to see what book this might be. With him now standing directly over it, he is baffled at what he sees.

Just before Aiden lies a copy of the old book his mother taught him to first read. He reaches down with a trembling hand and grabs hold of *Go, Dog*s! *Go!* He views it from cover to cover, noticing the perfect condition that it is in. Lost in the object that sits in his hands, he is unaware that the train doors have begun to close. It is not until the same light chime goes off that he notices. He attempts to dash towards the doors, but it is already too late. A sudden urge of panic overcomes Aiden as the train gradually inches forward. He feels himself about to scream but instantly stops himself when he takes a good look around the cart. He sees the walls and borders, normally used for ads and promotional objects, are filled with pictures and memories of his past. Photos that he recognizes from his father's house beautifully decorate the sides of the train.

As he continues to look on in amazement, Aiden starts to see pictures of his life, pictures that are impossible to exist. It is as though someone from above watched his every move and photographed it, knowing this moment would come. Aiden bounces from picture to picture while mixed emotions flutter throughout his being. He smiles and tears up while he views occasions with his mother, his best friend, his beautiful daughter and his gorgeous soulmate.

Lost in these moments, he has not even realized how quickly the train has been moving. He then removes his sights from the walls and to the window just in front of him. Blaring lights bolt by, one after the other, like giant fireflies in the night, catching his attention. His eyes try to lock on to each bulb flying by but his concentration is quickly snatched away as a certain reflection appears in the glass.

Aiden hurriedly spins around to view the seat just behind him. It is there that he sees a man sitting there. He begins to question whether this man has been there this entire time, or did he somehow magically appear? Aiden stares a little harder, coming to the realization that he knows exactly who this man is.

"Kenneth?" Aiden whispers.

The man's head instantly raises, revealing his face to be exactly who Aiden called out to.

"Hey, Aiden. It's good to finally see you again," Kenneth says. "It's just that I'm not who I appear to be."

"What do you mean?" Aiden questions, very confused.

"I mean, I'm not Kenneth."

"Okay… then why do you look like him?"

"I just assumed you'd feel better if you saw a familiar face rather than a face you didn't know."

"All right. And who are you exactly?"

"See. That part is a little tricky. I'm not really a who. More like a what, I guess you can say."

Unsure of what to even ask at this point, Aiden just stares on at the Kenneth imposter.

"I know this is all confusing. You're in a train with what seems to be your best friend, surrounded by memories of your life…" Kenneth pauses. "How's about you just take a seat for a moment? Enjoy the ride." He points to the seat opposite him.

Aiden turns to view the seat, nods in agreement and gently places his backside on the bench behind him. Feeling skeptical at what is currently taking place, he refuses to relinquish his vision from Kenneth's duplicate.

"Tell me, Aiden. What do you know about where you are?"

"I'm not sure I really know much of anything," Aiden replies.

"Okay. Then tell me what you think you know."

"I know that I'm not alive… but I'm also not dead? I think."

"Yeah. You are on the right track. No pun intended," he says, referencing the train.

"Wait, what about Tony?"

"What about him?"

"Where is he? What happened? We saw one of us about to…"

"None of that matters, Aiden. You two are on different paths. This one is yours and yours alone."

"And how do you know all of this? What are you?"

"I go by many names, Aiden. Some refer to me as The End, some call me the Reaper. But most just call me death."

"Then I am dead?" Aiden cries out.

"You're getting there."

Aiden leisurely stands to look over the being before him. His eyes fully submerge in tears while his hands begin to gently vibrate.

"Is this is some kind of trip to my afterlife and you're my tour guide? Is that it?"

"This place has many names. Many refer to it as limbo. But I call it the Parting Glass. That small space between the living and the dead. I know this is all too confusing for you. Just try to relax and allow yourself to sink into it."

"Relax? I can't relax. I'm being told I'm dead by death himself, who has disguised himself as my very best friend." Aiden pauses. "I can't be here! I have to get off this train. I have to go home."

"You're not going home, Aiden. There's still so much more you have to see."

Just then the train begins to slow down. The sound of the brakes coming down replaces the echoes of lights zooming by. Aiden swings his head around to now see what appears to be the break of dawn. The train has mysteriously left its tracks and placed itself onto a grassy field outside, blaring in the reddish-orange rays. The tracks casually come to a halt, causing the caboose to come to a standstill. The doors open, allowing Aiden to peer at the outside. The smell of freshly soaked grass accumulates inside his nose. It becomes apparent that wherever this train has brought him, it is no longer the wintery weather he was in earlier.

Aiden then turns around to call back to the imposter Kenneth but is astounded by the fact that he is no longer there. Somewhere along the way, death was able to sneak its way out while Aiden was caught up in the amazement of the mural-like atmosphere. Giving no second thought, he turns back around and takes his first steps off the train and is immediately met with the meadow and soil. Slowly he inches away from the cart doors and walks further and further onto the field. Suddenly a figure captures his attention. A figure that sits on a park bench off in the adjacent distance. At first, he is hesitant to approach until he captures a glimpse of yet another familiar face.

"Skylar? What are you doing here?" Aiden asks.

Skylar just smiles just before shaking her head, indicating that she is not who Aiden sees.

"You again, huh?"

"Yes. Me again is correct," Skylar responds. "Why don't you join me in yet another sit-down, Aiden?"

"Do I have a choice?"

"Of course you have a choice. But it's not like you're going anywhere, so you might as well humor me."

Quickly growing tired of these responses, Aiden distastefully nods his head and complies with the suggestion.

"Are you getting a kick out of pretending to be people that I know or are close to me?" Aiden questions.

"Like I've said, I thought it would be easier to speak to someone you already know," she replies.

"But you're not them."

"Ah. I see. Would you rather I do that whole traditional skeleton, black hood combo for you? I honestly find it quite distasteful."

Aiden turns his head and glares at the Skylar to his side.

"You see… I didn't think you would," she adds.

Aiden then begins to look around, taking notice of the location for the very first time.

"Why are we here?" Aiden asks.

"This is where you two first met. Where you swept her off her feet and she fell madly in love with you."

"What is the point of all this? Huh? Tell me."

"You seem bothered, Aiden. I thought this body and this memory might put you more at ease."

"I can't be at ease. This place isn't real. The bodies you dress up as are clearly not real. So, tell me, what is the point?"

"Aiden… Aiden… Aiden. You may not see it now, but you being here is a gift. It is something you are going to need."

Aiden tries to muster something to say — anything. But nothing is able to spew from his lips. His only response is to place his face in between his fingertips and gradually rub his temples while he waits for whatever is supposed to come next.

"It's a terrible thing to waste, Aiden," Skylar utters.

"Waste what? My life? I didn't waste my life," Aiden responds with his attention captured.

"No, not life. Love. Love is a terrible thing to waste," she says. "To selfishly tell someone you love them and never mean it... That is something much worse beyond me."

Aiden instantly feels his insides crawling around, dying to split through. His nerves begin to rattle, begging for his sympathy to reign free.

"I'm sorry! I am so sorry for that. You can never understand how sorry I truly am," he says with tears in his eyes.

"On the contrary, Aiden, I do understand. It is you who needs to understand. It is you who needs to forgive, not seek it."

"What does that mean?"

Before Aiden can receive a response, a thunderous burst releases from the train's horn. Aiden turns his vision over to the train, noticing that its engine has slowly begun to start up again.

"You better go, Aiden. You wouldn't want to miss your train."

Aiden promptly stands up, takes one last look at Skylar and proceeds to dash towards the doors he recently exited. As he draws near, they begin to shut. His feet start to skip steps, hurrying him along in hopes of not missing the train's departure. Aiden then springs forward, pivoting his body to the side, just making his way through the clashing doors. He harshly falls flat on the ground, causing a brutal thud. His first instinct is not to check for backlash from the fall but instead look around for any new passenger. This time he is alone.

He calmly picks himself up off the floor and is greeted by new photos circulating around the cart. Photos of his mother and father smiling together are ingrained into his mind. They are memories he cannot seem to remember, or he simply was never a part of. For some reason, there is one photo that calls to him. A photo he in fact recognizes. It is the photo of his graduation day, in which he stood side-by-side with his mother. He stretches out to it. His hand extends, gracefully gliding his fingertips over his mother's beautiful smile. He too smiles back, as though that very picture could see him.

Just as Aiden is being soaked into these memories, the train once again comes to a break. The sound of the mist spraying chimes in again, causing Aiden to turn. This time he isn't greeted with a ray of sunlight but a dark and ominous rain cloud that is gushing. Thunder and lightning clash in the foreground, causing the grey sky to convey the impression of purple. Knowing the manner of nature does not matter here, he graciously steps out onto the muddy terrain. He immediately begins to look for the new silhouette awaiting his arrival and it does not take long.

Just a few feet away, a larger physique stands. Larger than the previous ones. Without any hesitation this time around, Aiden strolls over to it and calls out, "Who are we this time?"

The figure turns on call and reveals the embodiment of Aiden's father, Hal.

"Hello, Aiden. Good to see you here once again."

"You know... I really don't have time for this shit."

"Time? What makes you think you are entitled to time?"

"Okay then, you tell me, DAD. What am I entitled to?"

"Forgiveness."

"Again, with that."

"You see. You are not getting it."

"So then why don't you just tell me?"

"Because for once, this is a lesson you have to learn all on your own."

"Fine! I forgive, okay? I forgive everyone for everything... Happy now?"

"It's really hard to believe that when this is the only time you've ever been here."

"Here? What's here? There's nothing here except—"

Aiden's words disappear into the sound waves of the crashing rain and the overly angry thunder. They quickly die out at the sight of Hal moving aside and unveiling the gravestone that belongs to none other than Aiden's mother. Unable to fathom what lies before him, Aiden continues to read the tombstone over and over, only to continuously be convinced whose stone it is. He instantaneously drops to his knees and cowers over the marble heading. The grieving tears falling from his face are easily disguised with the equally sorrowful rainfall.

"Why... why would you have me come here?" Aiden demands to know.

"Forgiveness, Aiden," Hal says. "You have held onto her death for all of these years, refusing to let it go. You have told yourself that you were to blame throughout your entire life, unwilling to accept it as an accident you just could not prevent from happening."

"I have accepted it."

"No, Aiden. You've only accepted that she is gone. But you have never forgiven yourself for it and that's why you have never visited your own mother's resting place. Because coming here would only prove to you what you fear most."

"And what's that?"

"That it is real and that it did happen."

"I'm well aware that this is real. I know that she's gone and there is nothing I can do to bring her back. But I know that there was something I could've done." He pauses. "I know that if I had been there, I could've saved her. But why do I need to tell you that? You were there, I'm sure."

"And you're all right with living that way?"

"Living? You call what I did living? No. I died the day that she died. I died when I realized my selfish wants were more beneficial to me than hers."

Hal, seeing the pain flourishing from Aiden's mind and lips, places his palm down upon Aiden's shoulder.

"And what of your daughter and Marie? You think that if you had been home to save your mother, you'd be alive and would still be presented with such beautiful gifts as them?"

"Don't you dare."

"I only speak the truth, Aiden. Sooner or later, you'll have to see it. You'll have to forgive."

The sound of an engine starting begins to overthrow the rain. Aiden lifts his head and sees the train about to go into motion. He comes off the ground and onto his feet. He does not bother to look back at his supposed father. He simply ignores those last remarks and strolls over to the familiar entrance way. He then enters, keeping his head down with his face professedly buried in his chest, refusing to acknowledge any new possible memories on the walls. He simply listens to the train take off as the wheels below clatter against what seem to be metal tracks. He shuts his eyes for just a moment, getting lost in the vibrations of steel.

Aiden can sense the sonorousness calming. The train is pulling into its final destination. His eyes open and are greeted by the night sky. A gentle wind brushes up against the glass, giving this twilight a gentle feel. It is then the doors open but this time without a single sound. Aiden steps forward onto an familiar street. He quickly looks around and instantly notices he is back home. The home in which his mother was killed. He thinks about re-entering the train but is immediately denied as the train's lights shut, followed by the engine. He reluctantly looks around at the street level as haunting memories resurface in his mind.

He has returned to a place he never wanted to, but this time it feels different. This time there are no police sirens or lights ablaze. There is no crowd piling up, craving to gather information. There is only Aiden, the whispering wind and a single light. A light shining from above, peeking through his old living room window. Though he is not inside his actual body, he can feel his heart begging to be ripped from his chest. His muscles grow weak from anxiousness. Unable to shake the feeling that this light is calling to him, Aiden finally takes his first step towards his old entryway.

Coming face-to-face with the first door, Aiden gently pushes it forward, allowing it to glide open. He slowly enters, still shaking from the thoughts of what might be awaiting him. He nudges himself forward and starts to climb the stairs. Each one feels like a mountain that is larger than the last. His childhood memories return almost in an instant as he draws closer. His front door, now inches away, calls for his subtle touch. His hand rocks back and forth just as he places his palm right up against it. With no effort from him at all, the door deliberately reveals the hallway. Coming this far, Aiden nudges himself in, reintroducing himself to all of his mother's old photos and collectibles. An innocent smile returns to Aiden's face while he weirdly says hello to all of these things he once knew.

No longer able to hear the howling wind, the only sound that transpires, is the sound of two book pages attempting to separate. Aiden diverges himself deeper and deeper into his home, and that is when he comes face-to-face with her. Sitting there in her favorite chair with Aiden's favorite book in hand is Samantha,

Aiden's mother. The two instantly take notice of one another, causing Aiden to freeze in time.

"Mom…" Aiden calls out.

"Hello, my baby boy," she replies.

"You're not her. You're not my mother."

"It's me, my baby. It's really me."

Without any doubt, Aiden believes it with everything in him.

"Mom!" Aiden shouts, dashing towards Samantha.

The two collide and grip one another, immediately suffocating in each other's tears.

"How… this isn't possible," Aiden cries.

"It is possible. It is."

Aiden sobs into his mother's arms, praying this moment is not a lie. But in no time, he is convinced that it is not. It is then his mother removes her son from her shoulder and grips his face, forcing him to look directly into her eyes. Both with eyes puffed and crimson, she begins to smother him with kisses just before saying, "My beautiful baby boy. You have grown so much. And you are so handsome."

Aiden cannot seem to place together the words he wants. Instead, he lets the tears speak for him and re-enters his mother's arms.

"I have missed you so much, mom," Aiden muffles through his tears on her shoulder.

"And I have missed you."

Reluctantly, Aiden slowly loosens his hold and takes just one step back.

"Come sit with me, Aiden. It's been so long."

Samantha gently grabs hold of Aiden's hand and leads him towards their old brown couch where Aiden learned to read. They simultaneously sit down, disallowing the other to let go.

"I still can't believe you're here," she says.

"I can't believe I'm here," Aiden replies.

"Tell me... how has my son been?"

"Miserable. Absolutely miserable without you."

"That can't totally be true, Aiden."

"It is, mom."

"Why, my baby? Talk to me."

And just like that, the truth hits Aiden like a seventy-storey building collapsing on itself. Everything in his facial expression changes. His eyes droop while his partial smile transforms into a sulking pout.

"Because you haven't been there. And it's my fault. It's all my fault."

"It is not your fault, baby."

"Yes, it is. Had I had been there..."

"It's okay..."

"It's not. That thing... was right. I have never accepted losing you. I have never forgiven dad for not being there. I have never forgiven myself. And honestly, I don't think I ever can."

Samantha sees the pain her son is carrying, and it hurts her deeply. It is destroying her to see her son this way.

"Listen to me..." she says, grabbing hold of his face. "This is not your fault. None of it is your fault. If you were there, they might have buried two bodies instead of just one... I need you to stop, Aiden. I need you to find a way to let all of this go and accept it. Most of all, I need you to forgive not only your father but yourself... The world is way too beautiful and great for you to live the way you have... Please, my baby boy, find it in your heart to forgive."

"How?"

"By allowing yourself to love and to be loved. By seeing it

in that beautiful granddaughter of mine. By knowing I have never left your side once. No matter how far away I may seem, no matter how long it has been, I am always there with you, Aiden. For the rest of your life."

"I know, mom. I know. I just miss you all the time."

"And I miss you. But it's time you live your life. Go live and love that beautiful Marie of yours. I have seen her, and she is gorgeous inside and out. Truly a good woman. One that could never compare to the woman I envisioned you with."

Aiden smiles while gripping onto his mother's hands, caressing them ever so gently.

"Can't I just stay with you?"

"Of course you can stay. I'd never make you leave, but this isn't where you are supposed to be. You have to understand that even though you leave here, I will never leave you." She pauses. "You can stay, Aiden, but you will never know love like you could. You'd have to watch your daughter from a distance as I have watched you. And I know you. You're not finished. I have watched you go from just a boy to a man in just a blink of an eye… and I have to say, I am so proud of you. I am so proud of the man and father you have become. The way you love that little girl is the same love I have with you. And you know deep down, it's not time to let that go."

Aiden simply nods at his mother's words, knowing all that she has said is the truth.

"Now come here, my baby," Samantha requests, scooting over to the corner of the couch.

Aiden just smiles and lays across his mother's lap. She gently begins rubbing her hands through Aiden's hair, just as she did when he was a boy.

"That's how you used to put me to sleep."

"You remember…"

"Of course I do. There's nothing about you I will ever forget."

"My Aiden… I love you so much."

"I love you too, mom."

Samantha continues to run her fingertips throughout her son's scalp. She looks down at him with a gleaming smile and simply asks, "Do you forgive yourself?"

"I do," he says with a single tear sliding down from his cheekbone.

"I hope so. Now get some rest, my baby. You've been running around all day. I'll be here when you wake up."

As Samantha continues her tender embrace, Aiden can feel his eyes grow heavier. The world around is finally one of peace. He can feel each strand of hair bouncing between her fingers with every cultivating swipe. The air begins to cool down, leaving a pleasurable aftermath. Aiden can feel himself drifting away into a peaceful slumber, and as much as he tries to fight it, it easily overtakes him. He has lost every battle to his mother's compassion and this one is no different. He takes one last look at the ceiling he's stared at so many times before he finally succumbs to slumber and drifts away into the black.

"You can open your eyes now, my baby boy," Samantha says no sooner than when he shuts his eyes.

On those words, Aiden's eyes catapult open. An unfamiliar, bland ceiling greets him. It is not the one from his home but one he's never seen before. He tries to understand where he is or what is happening until an angelic voice speaks.

"Triple A baseball superstar, Tony Garcia, sadly passed away earlier this week, after being taken off life support. He will be remembered for his outstanding talents on the field and his amazing contributions to many charitable organizations. Mr Garcia was a man recognized for many donations, but none more important than his most recent. In the wake of his death, Mr Garcia had many of his organs donated, such as his kidneys and heart, so that others may live," Marie reads from a newspaper, sitting at Aiden's beside.

"God, you're beautiful," Aiden barely utters.

Marie's pupils spring open. The newspaper in her hands falls to the ground. Her jaw instantly drops as she stares into Aiden's barely blinking eyes. Unsure of what to do, she gently shakes, smiles and rises from her chair.

"Aiden... Aiden!" she declares.

She makes her way over to his side and sits next to him on the bed. Her rattling hands carefully caress the sides of his face, trying to convince herself that this moment is real. The two just glare at one another in love as they have done so many times before.

"I love you, I love you, I love you," Marie repeats.

"Did I finally make it to heaven?" Aiden asks.

"Why would you think that?"

"Because you're clearly the angel that God sent me."

"Smooth," she says, crying tears of joy.

Marie gracefully snuggles into Aiden's arms, holding him as though she has not seen him in a thousand lifetimes. She sobs into his torso, finally able to reconnect with the man she loves. She places her hands all over his body, making sure this is truly happening and isn't just another fantasy world. She listens for his heart as his chest slightly lifts to the air with each breath he takes. Not able to withstand no longer looking at his handsome grin, Marie props her head up and attends to his glance.

"I love you, Marie," he says.

"I love you more," she replies.

"For the rest of our lives?"

"For the rest of our lives!"

The couple continue to be cemented in this moment. It is the moment they have lived for, the moment they died for and the moment they escaped death for. They had to travel worlds unknown for this love. Now there is nothing else in their way. They are forever mated by their souls.

Epilogue
Face Tomorrow As We Say Goodbye to Yesterday

Weeks have passed since their tragic accident. The days and nights have grown a bit colder, but for Aiden and Marie they have somehow become warmer. Their love has been ignited like no other, cherishing each day side by side. Together they walk amongst the dead, this time a part of the living, passing headstone after headstone. Aiden is barely able to walk on his own, so he clutches tightly to his walking cane while Marie guides his hobble. They make their way over to a familiar place, pushing against a very demanding gust of wind. Aiden turns to Marie, gives her a nod, then a kiss and continues for a moment on his own.

He struggles a bit with his cane, unable to grip onto the stale grass, but he makes do. He finally reaches the destination he wishes for and places his cane off to the side and goes down to a single knee. He steadily places his hand upon the gravestone before him and places down a bouquet of roses. He forcibly inhales a sigh of pain and firmly exhales one of relief. He then closes his eyes for just a moment, inhales once more and opens them back up before reciting, "Hi, mom…"

Aiden has finally come to his mother's resting place. Filled with excitement and sentiment, Aiden stares at her name, instantly getting lost in the moment. He pictures his mother sitting there just as they did that night a few weeks back. He imagines being able to gaze into his mother's beautiful eyes once more. He remembers her every word and knows that even though her body is not near him, she is very much with him on this occasion.

"It's me, Aiden. But of course, you already know that," he states. "I never thought in a million years I would ever actually come here, but I had to. I wanted to." He pauses to clear his throat. "I wanted to come here to tell you that I'm doing well. Marie is doing good. Kenneth too. He says hi, by the way... Anyway, I wanted to come and have one of our talks and let you know that these days haven't really been easy, but they sure as hell are getting there. I think about you every day. And each time that I do, I listen to the wind or the snow or the rain and I know that you're there, calling out to me. I think about how you've always helped me even when I wasn't even sure if you did... I wanted to tell you how much I love you and how much I miss you... and how much I thank you for everything."

Aiden's gentle cry begins to fall upon the earth as he pauses to wipe away his delicate tears.

"I also wanted you to be the first to know that I'm planning on proposing to Marie... with your ring, if that's okay. I'm sure that's okay with you or else someone would have come to haunt me by now." He chuckles. "I also wanted you to know that I plan on reserving you a seat... I know you wouldn't miss it... You'll be right there, front row, giving your blessing."

Suddenly a beautiful and gentle voice calls out to Aiden.

"Daddy!" little Marie calls out, standing there with her mother and Marie.

Aiden turns his head away from his mother for just a moment and smiles the most marvelous smile.

"I almost forgot. Marie met Marie. I know that sounds funny... but it is amazing. And Skylar has been nothing but amazing about it. You know, for the first time, I feel like the world isn't such a bad place, and I have you to thank for it."

"Daddy. Can I come?" Marie requests.

Aiden just glimmers with excitement and calls his daughter over. She immediately sprints over to her father and dives right into his arms, relinquishing her childish laugh. Aiden slightly groans from the pain but brushes it off, because there is no amount of discomfort that can add up to this loving embrace.

"Be careful, Marie," Skylar calls out.

"It's okay," Aiden yells back.

Aiden grins a large grin and pulls his daughter in close.

"Mom... there's someone I'd love you to meet. This is Marie, your granddaughter. She's beautiful and smart... and has that good old family attitude," Aiden says with a laugh. "Marie, this is your grandma."

Without being told or given instruction, Marie looks down upon the stone and says, "Hi, grandma. I'm Marie."

"Isn't she gorgeous, mom?"

Aiden and Marie share a gentle hug before a simple kiss is placed upon her cheek.

"Can you go back to mommy for just a second? I just want to say goodbye to grandma."

"Okay, daddy."

Marie runs back to her mother immediately after her father's request. He then turns back to the gravestone to finish his conversation.

"You know, mom, had you told me a year ago I'd be here with all the women I love, I would have called you crazy..."

Suddenly, a light buzzing noise goes off in Aiden's pocket. He swiftly reaches in and pulls his cellphone out. He looks down at the screen and smiles once more at his mother.

"I guess this is my cue, mom." He pauses. "I just want to say thank you again. You'll always be the true love of my life... I miss you... and I love you..."

Aiden places his fingertips to his lips, lightly pushing a kiss up against them. He then proceeds to place his hand up to his mother's name and gracefully taps the stone. He then uses that same hand and swipes the phone screen to answer his call and places it up to his ear.

"Hey, dad... Yup, we are actually on the way now... we will see you soon."

Still on the phone, Aiden rises and begins to walk away. Just behind the headstone, Samantha's spirit watches on, smiling. She gracefully stares at her son walk away and rejoin his family's side. It is this moment she prayed for each day. This is the only thing she has ever truly wanted for her son, and now he has it. She senses the true love and peace amongst them, which can finally allow her to rest at ease.

Samantha begins to shine with a glorious light as she smiles once more at her son.

"I love you too, my baby boy," she says, bidding farewell for now.

Her words are instantly carried through the air and into Aiden's ear. He smoothly turns around, taking one more look. He simply smiles and nods, knowing he will never be alone again. He then turns back, wrapping his arms around both of Marie's, finally able to know what true love is. Together, they all laugh and fill the atmosphere with joy. Together, they enter a new world of peaceful bliss.